"Take me inside," he murmured against her throat.

For a hectic moment, Lisa didn't know whether he meant her home or her body. Or both. And, crazily, did not care. She almost agreed to let him in and go wherever it took her....

But then she opened her eyes. Behind his head she saw the elegant sweep of the terrace, the chauffeur-driven car. A cold thought struck: this is a rich man playing a game. A clever game but a game nonetheless. She had been there before and it hurt.

Nikolai felt her turn to a block of wood in his arms. He raised his head and let her go.

"You change your mind fast," Nikolai said.

"No, I don't. I've always said I didn't want to have anything to do with you." To her own astonishment she sounded quite cool about it.

"Are you denying you wanted me just now?"

The streets of London aren't just paved with gold—they're home to three of the world's most eligible bachelors!

London, England: a city of style, sophistication—and romance! Its exclusive Notting Hill district is the perfect place to fall in love. Sparks fly as three sexy, single men meet—and marry?—three lively, independent women....

This fabulous miniseries features the talents of **Sara Craven, Mary Lyons and Sophie Weston:** three hugely popular authors who between them have sold more than 35 million books worldwide.

Notting Hill Grooms:

2000 Launch!
Irresistible Temptation by Sara Craven #2077

On sale Jan. 2000:
Reform of the Playboy by Mary Lyons #2083

On sale Feb. 2000:
The Millionaire Affair by Sophie Weston #2089

SOPHIE WESTON

The Millionaire Affair

NOTTING HILL GROOMS

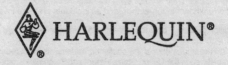

HARLEQUIN®

TORONTO • NEW YORK • LONDON
AMSTERDAM • PARIS • SYDNEY • HAMBURG
STOCKHOLM • ATHENS • TOKYO • MILAN • MADRID
PRAGUE • WARSAW • BUDAPEST • AUCKLAND

ISBN 0-373-12089-3

THE MILLIONAIRE AFFAIR

First North American Publication 2000.

Copyright © 1999 by Sophie Weston.

PROLOGUE

THE overheated ballroom was heady with the scent of hot house lilies. The party had got to the stage of slow dancing. In clouds of figured satin the bride was circling in the arms of the most glamorous man in the room.

A photographer, indistinguishable in his dinner jacket from the elegant guests, pointed his camera at the couple.

'Bride and Count Nikolai Ivanov,' he murmured to his assistant.

'Exposure ninety-eight: Ivanov,' she wrote down obediently.

She peered over the top of her notebook.

Count Nikolai Ivanov was well over six feet, with midnight-dark hair, broad shoulders and an unambiguous self-confidence that hit you between the eyes. Add to that the haughty profile of an Aztec prince, and eyes at once intense and alert with sophisticated amusement, and it was no wonder that the bride was gazing up at him, mesmerised. When he swung her into the air with an easy strength, the assistant sighed.

'Wow,' she said, appreciative and envious. 'Now why haven't I seen him before?'

'Wouldn't have done you any good if you had.' The photographer continued to rake the room with his lens. 'Most eligible bachelor in Europe and he spends half his time in the jungle. Terrible waste. Not your style at all.'

'Oh, I could stretch a point in this case,' said the assistant with feeling. 'He's *gorgeous*.'

Her boss looked at her cynically. 'He's also a heartbreaker. And the last of his line since his brother died.'

5

'I wasn't thinking of trying to marry the man,' protested the girl, laughing.

'Just as well. The Ivanovs can trace their line further than the Romanovs, I'm told. Count Nikolai won't be marrying anyone unless she has at least three coats of arms and a title in the family.' He raised his camera again. 'Ah, there's the mother of the bride with our hostess. Exposure ninety-nine: Madame Repiquet and Countess Ivanova.'

'Grandmère is looking tired,' Nikolai murmured in his grandfather's ear. 'Shall I take her away?'

'You can try,' said his grandfather humorously.

Véronique Repiquet was lucky to be allowed to hold her wedding reception in this exquisite French château. The revels, as everyone knew, would go on all night. So it had been arranged that the old Count and Countess would spend the night at Nikolai's small villa on the estate.

His grandson chuckled. 'I shall take a firm line,' he said confidently. 'Women always respond to that.'

His grandfather cast his eyes to the magnificent gilded ceiling.

'You think you know so much about women, don't you?'

'I'm an animal behaviourist,' said Nikolai with a twinkle. 'I've been trained to know about women.'

His grandfather smiled. But he looked perturbed as well.

'Do you never have any doubts, Nicki?'

Nikolai looked startled. 'All the time. Every expedition, every paper I write, every lecture I give. If I didn't have any doubts there wouldn't be anything interesting left to research.'

'I didn't mean about your work,' snapped his grandfather, suddenly annoyed. 'I meant about women.'

Nikolai looked at him in concern. The loss of temper was out of character for his gentle grandfather. He slipped his arm round the older man's shoulders.

'What is it, Pauli? Regretting lending the château for this junket?'

The older man shook his head. 'No,' he said on a half-sigh. 'No. But your grandmother was saying—it should have been Vladi's wedding.'

For a moment Nikolai's expression was stark. Pauli cursed himself for his clumsiness. Vladi had been killed a year ago, but sometimes he wondered whether Nikolai was over his brother's death even yet.

He said hurriedly, 'Still, it's good to see her enjoying herself again. I thought a big party might be too much for her. But she said it would be good practice for your wedding.'

'Ouch,' said Nikolai. His expression was half-rueful, half-sad.

His grandfather did not pretend to misunderstand him.

'Why are you so set against marriage, Nicki?'

Nikolai looked round at the crowded room. The music had started again, louder and heavier now that the older guests were leaving. Men threw off their hot jackets. Girls bared their shoulders and let their elaborate hairstyles fall as they would. Nikolai grimaced.

'Maybe I'm just not a party animal.'

His grandfather was not deflected. 'You can party with the best of them when you want. Anyway, marriage is more than a party.'

'Exactly.'

Pauli peered up at his tall grandson. 'Are you *afraid* of marriage, Nicki?'

Nikolai looked away. The firm mouth set into a stubborn line.

He knew that expression, thought Pauli. The shutters had come down. Normally he would have stopped there. But tonight, for some reason, he kept on.

'We've never asked. You like your privacy and we've never wanted to intrude. But—have you ever lived with a woman, Nicki?'

Nikolai's eyes flickered. He gave his grandfather a wide, false smile and shuddered dramatically. 'Never.'

'But there have been women,' said Pauli, revealing that even if he didn't ask he had other ways of finding out what he wanted to know.

'Of course there have been women,' said Nikolai calmly. 'I just don't let them move in.'

'But—'

'It only encourages them. Once a woman hangs her clothes in your wardrobe, she thinks she's got rights in you.'

Pauli's expression darkened. He turned his head away so Nikolai could not see it.

'You sound very cold-hearted.'

'That's me,' said Nikolai cheerfully. 'Hot blood. Cold heart. Makes for a peaceful life.'

CHAPTER ONE

'So FIRE me!'

Lisa Romaine tilted her pointed chin to a challenging angle. She leaned insolently against the wall, looked her boss straight in the eye and waited.

Behind his desk, Sam Voss shifted irritably. 'Can't I give my Head of Bond Trading a hint?'

'Hint!'

He tried a winning smile. 'Now, Lisa, don't overreact. Why don't you sit down and we can talk?'

Predictably, she did not move. Her green eyes narrowed to slits.

'Not about my private life,' she said dangerously.

'When you work for Napier Kraus, merchant bank to the new industrialists, you don't have a private life.'

Lisa looked ironic. 'You might not,' she said. 'I do.'

Sam shook his head. 'I thought you wanted to get on.'

'Sure,' said Lisa evenly. 'That's why I work hard and deliver the goods. I'm not going to turn myself inside out trying to be a clone of the managing director.'

'That's enough.' Sam's voice hardened. 'You're on the management team now. If you want to stay there, act like it.'

'At work, of course. But I'm not going to change my whole lifestyle. *And* turn my back on my friends.'

'Look, kid—'

'I'm twenty-two,' flashed Lisa, suddenly losing her cool. 'Don't patronise me.'

'Then stop digging your heels in. You're a clever girl and you deserve your chance. Don't blow it.'

'What do you mean?'

'I mean the Personnel Committee aren't sure about you,' he told her brutally.

'Why? With my score—'

'Oh, they like your results,' he allowed. 'You're up there on the shortlist for Trader of the Year. Of course they like your results. They're just not sure about a woman bossing a lot of punchy guys.'

Lisa gave a scornful shrug, not answering.

'And, frankly, they're not sure about your image either,' said Sam, goaded.

'What's wrong with my image?'

He waved a hand. 'You're a good-looking kid. Sorry— woman. Get yourself a decent haircut and couple of designer suits and you could be in there mixing it with the MBA dollies. God knows, you're bright enough. So why go out of your way to look like a punk?'

Lisa looked down her nose. Sam lost no chance to put her down, but on the issue of her appearance she was quite confident. The glass wall behind his desk reflected an image back at her which no one but Sam had any problems with: natural blonde hair, gamine features, long legs in spite of her moderate height and a figure to die for. It had taken all her considerable personality to stop her new staff from wolf-whistling at her every time she left her desk. 'I don't look like a punk,' she said calmly.

Sam was alone in Napier Kraus in his lack of appreciation of Lisa's black-clad legs. Even the Financial Controller had been known to give them a passing beam. Now Sam glared at her short skirt.

'One day soon you're going to find yourself hosting one of our corporate entertainments. How are the clients going to feel being taken to the races by a woman with earrings like a modern art gallery?'

Lisa put her hand to one of the offending ornaments.

'You're not serious!'

'The top brass already know you live in a place that's

one up from a student squat. The chauffeurs talk, you know.'

Lisa was outraged. Her eyes were usually a green flecked with the gold of a woodland summer. Now they were green ice. 'You're a snob.'

'No. I just know the score.' He was torn between affection and exasperation. 'Face it, Lisa. We've got a parent company with some very definite ideas about how it wants its management to live. You don't qualify on any count.'

Lisa folded her arms across her chest and glared. 'And to qualify I've got to pretend to be something I'm not?'

'Up to you,' said Sam, losing patience. 'Now get out of here and make us some money.'

It was the end of a bad week. With Far Eastern markets in freefall, Lisa had had to be at her desk earlier than ever, staying well after New York had closed for transatlantic strategy discussions, and she hadn't got home until after ten.

As a result, she'd missed her turn to clean the shared kitchen. But what had really offended her housemates was her failure to make it to Anna's twenty-first on Wednesday evening.

'Too grand to remember something like a birthday party now,' Alec Palmer had sneered.

Of all the people she shared the house with, Alec was the one who knew most about her job. He had even worked at Napier Kraus briefly himself. When he'd first moved into the house they had got on well. But since her promotion he had sniped constantly.

In a way, she could understand it. He was older and, unlike Lisa, who had left school at sixteen, he had a university degree. It was natural that he would feel competitive. But there was an edge of spite in his remarks these days that Lisa found hard to bear.

Maybe I should do what Sam wants and move out, thought Lisa. She hated the idea of giving in to what she thought of as snobbery. But if Alec was going to pick at

her all the time, she would be better off living somewhere
else.

So her heart sank when she went into the kitchen that
night and found Alec was the only one home. He was standing at the stove, stirring onions into a Bolognese sauce.

'The others have gone clubbing,' he said, his back to her.
'They said they were going to try to get into the Equinox
Club. You could always catch them up.'

Lisa tossed her briefcase onto a kitchen chair.

'Frankly, I can do with a quiet night. It's been a pig of a
week.'

'The burdens of responsibility,' said Alec, with an edge
to his voice.

Lisa tensed. But he waved his spatula at the pan of boiling
pasta.

'Want some spaghetti?'

Lisa seized the olive branch gratefully. 'That would be
great. Just let me change.'

She went and had a quick shower, then pulled on jeans
and a sloppy shirt and went back to the kitchen.

Alec had set the table and opened a bottle of red wine.
Lisa sank onto a pine chair. She took the glass he offered
her and raised it to him in a silent toast.

'This is a real treat. Thanks, Alec.'

'Pleasure.'

He dished up and put the plate in front of her. She grated
some parmesan onto the meat sauce and began to eat hungrily.

At first it was easy. They talked about the food, plans for
the weekend, families. Even work, carefully. But then Lisa
asked idly, 'Is Equinox part of the on-going birthday cele-
brations?' and Alec blew up.

'You've got no right to sneer.'

'I wasn't—'

'A six-figure salary doesn't make you better than the rest
of us.'

Lisa sighed. As far as her housemates were concerned

she was an East End kid made good: irrepressible, hard-working, quick on the draw. None of them knew the hours of work it had cost her, or the loneliness. And not one of them even suspected the private burden of the responsibilities she carried.

'I'm too tired for this, Alec.'

He gave a bitter laugh. *'Too tired,'* he mimicked savagely. 'A big job is all-consuming, isn't it? I suppose I should be grateful that you had the time to eat my food tonight.'

Lisa winced. But she said indignantly, 'Garbage.'

He stood up and came round the table, looking down at her broodingly. 'When did you last have time for me?'

'Alec—'

He seemed not to hear. He searched her face.

'You don't even see it, do you?'

His own face twisted. For a horrible moment, Lisa thought he was going to cry. She winced away from his too revealing expression, but it was too late. He had seen her distaste. He grabbed her up from her chair.

'Look at me, Lisa.' Suddenly he was a stranger, panting and desperate. 'Please. *Please.* I love you. No one loves you like I do.'

Lisa was appalled. It came out of the blue. The house had an agreement: no relationships between tenants. She had thought of Alec as a friend, and, lately, as a self-selected competitor she would have to treat carefully. It had never occurred to her that he was in love with her. She had no idea what to do.

'Don't say that,' she begged.

But he wasn't listening. He held onto her like a lifeline.

It pressed all the wrong buttons for Lisa. She had been vulnerable and in love herself. The sight of Alec's vulnerability twisted her heart. *I can't bear it,* she thought.

'Let me go.'

She struggled to free herself. He didn't seem to notice.

'You think you're so strong,' he muttered into her hair.

'But you need love. Everyone needs love. I can give you love.'

And, to Lisa's inexpressible horror, he slid down on one knee and pressed his face into her stomach.

'Alec, please don't do this.' It was a cry of real pain.

She pushed at his shoulders. But his grip was like a vice. Lisa looked round, helpless, hurting, and acutely embarrassed. He seemed unaware of his own strength. Or the fact that she was trying to get away.

Lisa stood very still and held her breath. Keep calm, she told herself. She had deflected plenty of over-enthusiastic guys in her time. This was just another one, for all his anguish. She just had to keep calm and stay discouraging but kind. He would stop in a minute. And then they could be friends again.

Who was she kidding? They could never be friends again. Not when he had let her see his feelings naked like this. Lisa leaned away from him, wincing.

Alec didn't notice that she was discouraging him. Intent on his own feelings, he was oblivious of hers. He began to tug at the fabric of her shirt. Whether to get it off or to pull her down onto the floor, was not clear. He kept muttering, like a mantra, 'I love you, I love you, I love you...'

Lisa's heart leaped in primitive disgust. She tore herself away.

'*Love,*' she spat.

That was when Alec looked up at her at last. There was a gleam of anger in his eyes, along with the tears. He came lithely to his feet and took hold of her. His lips were clumsy, suffocating, desperate.

Lisa closed her eyes. She was torn between pity and simple horror. She tried to push him away but he was too intent to pay any attention to her resistance. She wasn't even sure he noticed. It was faintly ludicrous, this pretend battle with a man she had thought of as a friend for more than three years. She jerked out of his hold.

'But I *love* you,' he repeated insistently, as indignant as if she had shot him.

He had stirred up old memories he had no idea of, and, between them, Alec and the memories had shaken Lisa to her core. They left her too upset to remember to be kind.

'Love. Huh! Don't insult my intelligence,' she said, retreating behind the table. 'You want to get into my bed and you think saying you love me will do it. Well, I've got news for you. That doesn't work with me. Not any more.'

'Lisa—' He was full of despair. And the beginnings of anger. He advanced on her with unmistakable purpose.

Lisa stopped even trying to spare his feelings. 'Don't *touch* me,' she cried.

She ran.

The next morning she got out of the house before anyone else was up. She toyed with the idea of going to her mother's. And rapidly discarded it. Joanne would say that she had enough problems dealing with Kit. Lisa was supposed to be the strong one, the one who found her own solutions.

In the end she went to the dance studio in Ladbroke Grove. There was an early class in jazz dance. Lisa flung herself into it.

With such effect, indeed, that as they left the studio at the end one of the other dancers said to her, 'And who were you trying to kill?'

'What?' Lisa looked round. 'Oh, hi, Tatiana. I didn't know you did jazz dance.'

Tatiana Lepatkina must be over seventy years old, but she still taught a ballet class at the centre. She and Lisa had bumped into each other first at an enthusiastic salsa session over a year ago. Now they strolled along to the changing room together.

'Dance!' sniffed Tatiana. 'What you were doing wasn't dance. That was pure combat training.'

For the first time since Alec's pounce, Lisa laughed.

Tatiana grinned. She was small and astringent. She was also something of a guru to the younger studio members, though no one actually knew how old she was. She had muscles like an athlete's and wore full dramatic make-up at all times. Even after she had showered it remained untouched.

Now they both stripped off and went into shower cubicles.

'I wouldn't have wanted to come within catching distance of your elbows. Or your feet, for that matter.'

She went silent for several minutes under the whooshing of water. When she emerged, wrapped in a huge white towel, Lisa was already dressed and combing her damp hair in the mirror. Tatiana put her head on one side, eyes bright with inquisitiveness.

'You are so lucky, with hair like that. Pure gold and natural too.' She added without a break, 'Who were you kicking this morning?'

Lisa raised an eyebrow at her reflection. 'Was it that obvious?'

Tatiana nodded. 'A man, I suppose?'

'Or two,' said Lisa, only half joking.

'Sounds complicated,' said Tatiana, pleased. 'Let's have something decaffeinated and you can tell me all about it.'

Rather to her surprise, Lisa found herself doing exactly that. When she had finished, Tatiana looked at her in silence for a moment, narrow-eyed.

'And you're sure you gave this man no encouragement?'

'Alec?' Lisa sighed. 'I've never thought so. We all had this agreement right from the start—no inter-house affairs. Everyone stuck to it.'

There was an ironic pause. After a moment Lisa flung up her hands in a token of surrender.

'OK. OK. I *thought* everyone had stuck to it.'

'You can't make rules about feelings,' Tatiana said largely. 'Never works.'

Lisa looked mulish.

'Believe me,' Tatiana insisted. 'When I was still dancing, we used to be on tour for months at a time. You always start off saying no attachments. But human nature wins every time.'

Lisa said something very rude about human nature.

'No point in fighting it, though,' Tatiana pointed out practically. 'So—what are you going to do?'

Lisa sighed. 'Look for somewhere else to live. Alec will never forgive me, and I—well, frankly I'm not too proud of the way I handled it. I got in a panic, I suppose. All that *passion.*' And she pulled a face.

Tatiana, who was rather in favour of passion, was intrigued. 'Attracted in spite of yourself?'

Lisa was startled. 'Not a chance. Men are such idiots.'

'Oh.'

'I had my drama when I was eighteen,' said Lisa grandly. 'I got over it and grew up. Why can't they?'

Entertained, Tatiana murmured something about human nature again. Lisa frowned.

'Well, it's a terrible bore. Now I'll have to go house-hunting and I haven't got the time. What's more, my boss will start nagging me about getting what he calls a *suitable address*, and I almost certainly won't have the money for that without mortgaging my underwear. And anyway, I just *hate* doing what my boss tells me.'

'Ah.'

Tatiana was not only a teacher of ballet, she was a choreographer. Listening to Lisa, she had begun to perceive the story of a ballet. Now here was the dramatic *pas de deux:* the powerful man, the woman who fights him because she cannot admit the attraction between them.

'What's wrong with your boss?' she said carefully.

Lisa was savage suddenly. 'He doesn't like it that a woman has the best trading results in the room. He couldn't get out of promoting me, but he compensated by—' Just the thought of Sam's lecture made her choke with rage.

Tatiana made a few editorial amendments to her scenario.

'Did he suggest you say thank you in the traditional way?'

'What?' Lisa looked blank for a moment. Then she understood. 'Oh, no. He wouldn't dare make a pass at me.'

Looking at her pugnacious chin, Tatiana could believe it. 'So what did he do, then?'

'He gave me a lecture on my style. *Style!* I made half the portfolio's profits last quarter and he complains about my style!'

Tatiana was disappointed. She liked more passion in her drama. 'What is wrong with your style?'

Lisa listed the points on her fingers. 'Wrong address. Wrong clothes. Wrong friends.'

Tatiana began to see that this was a satisfactory drama after all.

'He thinks you are not good enough for him,' she deduced. She was indignant.

'In bucketfuls,' agreed Lisa. A shadow crossed her face. 'And he's not the first,' she added, almost to herself.

Tatiana didn't notice. She was thinking. 'Do you want to rent or buy?'

'Well, I'm renting at the moment—'

'Because you could always have the garden flat in my house. As long as you aren't determined to buy.'

'—but I don't want to have to go through—' Lisa realised what Tatiana had said. 'What?'

Tatiana repeated it obligingly.

Lisa shook her head, stunned. 'I didn't know—I mean I didn't realise—I wasn't fishing...' she said, acutely embarrassed.

Tatiana was amused. 'I know you weren't. Why should you? You don't know where I live, or that I have a flat to let.'

'No,' agreed Lisa, still slightly dazed.

'Well, I have. Just round the corner from here.' She paused impressively. 'Stanley Crescent.'

'Oh,' said Lisa.

Tatiana waited expectantly. It was clear that something more was required. Lisa had no idea what. She felt helpless.

Seeing her confusion, Tatiana smiled. 'It's a very good address.'

'Is it? I mean—I'm sure it is.' Lisa was floundering. She said desperately, 'I just don't know much about this part of London.'

'Secret gardens,' said Tatiana in thrilling tones.

'Sorry?'

'When you walk through Notting Hill all you see are these great white terraces on both sides of the street, right?'

'Right,' said Lisa, puzzled.

'Well, what you don't know is that behind several terraces there are huge communal gardens. Big as a park, some of them. Mature trees, rose gardens, the lot. It's like having a share of a house in the country.'

She waved her hands expressively. Quite suddenly, Lisa could see green vistas, trees in spring leaf, birds building nests, *space*. She gave a sigh of unconscious longing.

'Like gardens, do you?' said Tatiana, pleased.

'Never had one. Don't know,' said Lisa.

But her dreaming eyes told a different story. Tatiana took a decision.

'Move in on Monday.'

Lisa did.

It was a blustery day that blew the cherry blossom off the trees in a snowstorm of petals. Fortunately she didn't have much to move. She installed her boxes in the sitting room of Tatiana's garden flat, paid the movers and took a cab to work. She was at her desk by eleven.

She was greeted by a teasing cheer.

'Hey, hey, half a day's work today?' said Rob, her second in command.

'I moved house,' Lisa answered briefly. She settled behind her desk and tapped in her access code.

Rob's eyebrows climbed. Lisa had told him, raging, about her lecture from Sam on Friday afternoon.

'You don't hang about, do you?'

She was scrolling through the position pages on the screen but she looked up at that. Her wicked grin flashed.

'No sooner the word than the deed, me.'

'Sam will be impressed.'

Lisa chuckled naughtily. 'I know. But I can't help that.'

'I bet he checks up,' Rob mused. 'Just to make sure you've got a proper up-market place this time.'

Her laughter died. 'He wouldn't dare.'

'Want to bet?'

'If he does,' said Lisa with grim satisfaction, 'he's in for a surprise.'

For Lisa, too, the move turned out to have its surprises. For one thing she had the greatest difficulty in getting Tatiana to name a figure for the rent. Her new landlady had escorted her enthusiastically through the house—stuffed with an eclectic collection of furniture, ferns and *objets d'art*—the garden—as green and private as Lisa had imagined—and the local shops—everything from a late-night grocer's to a bookshop which sold nothing except books about food and even smelled like a good kitchen. There was no doubt that Tatiana was delighted to welcome her. But she clearly thought anything to do with money was low and wouldn't be pinned down on it.

'Look,' said Lisa, turning up at Tatiana's door one evening with a bottle of expensive Rioja, some information from the local estate agent and an expression of determination, 'this can't go on. You need a contract and so do I.'

She threw down a printed document onto a walnut sofa table which gleamed softly under an art deco lamp.

'That's a standard form. I've signed it but run it past your solicitor before you sign.' Something in Tatiana's expression gave her pause. 'You have got a solicitor?'

'The family has,' said Tatiana, without enthusiasm.

'Fine. Call him tomorrow. The one thing that I haven't

put in is the amount of rent. Now, the agent gave me a range for one-bedroomed flats in this area.' A handful of leaflets joined the contract. 'Pick one.'

Tatiana wrinkled her nose disdainfully. 'When I was your age, girls did not admit that they knew money existed. It was men's business.'

Lisa was not deflected from her purpose, but she grinned. 'Don't wriggle. I'm not leaving until I've given you a cheque.'

Tatiana picked up one of the estate agent's pages and looked at it with distaste. 'That's far too much. Anyway, that one's got a separate entrance.'

Lisa had come prepared. 'All right. There are monthly rentals for nine flats there. I've worked out the average.' She magicked a slip of paper out of her jeans pocket.

Tatiana took it gingerly. Lisa laughed. She had seen her look at a snail on the garden path with much the same shrinking distaste.

'Talk to your solicitor, or I'm moving out. And that would be a pity. This is a lovely place.'

The May evening was dark. From Tatiana's first-floor window the shadowed sweep of trees and lawns looked like a magic landscape. Lisa sank into a 1920s chaise longue under the window and sighed with pleasure.

'Wonderful,' she said exuberantly. 'I've never known anywhere like it.

Tatiana's eyes were warm. 'I'm glad.' She opened the wine and poured them each a glass. 'My family bought the house for me years ago. They thought if I could not, after all, make my living dancing, then at least I could rent out rooms.'

Lisa accepted the glass of ruby wine. 'And did you?'

'I've done both. Dancing is a hard life. Especially when you begin to age. These days I direct, but it was tough in my forties.' Tatiana frowned. 'My family still do an annual check-up, though.'

Lisa sipped wine, amused. 'Who's brave enough to do that?'

Tatiana sniffed. 'Well, this year it will probably be my nephew, Nikolai. Couldn't be more unsuitable. The last time I saw him he was wearing a beard and khaki camouflage gear. Still,' she added grudgingly, 'that was on television.'

'What a glamorous family.'

'Nikolai isn't glamorous,' corrected Tatiana. She had standards in the matter of glamour. 'He's an explorer. Writes books on the behaviour of primates.'

Lisa's eyes danced. 'A bit of a wild man, then?'

'Good heavens, no,' said his fond aunt. 'Not a wild bone in his body. He's always completely in control of himself.'

'But?' prompted Lisa, hearing the reservation in her voice.

'He wants to control everyone else as well,' announced Tatiana. 'And then thinks you should be delighted that he has bothered to give you so much of his attention. *Men.*'

Lisa had no men in her family, but she had been battling her way through a man's world ever since she first went to work for Napier Kraus. She could only sympathise.

'Still,' said Tatiana brightening, 'he came over just before Christmas, so I should have another six months before he starts trying to interfere again.'

She was wrong.

Nikolai Ivanov was as reluctant to involve himself in his great-aunt's affairs as she was to let him.

'Oh, not London again,' he told his grandfather.

They were walking up from the stables to the back of the château, gleaming like gold in the spring sunshine. The gentle slopes of the Tarn valley scrolled away like a medieval painting towards the river. The vine-clad landscape hadn't changed since his ancestor had commissioned a picture of his home in the eighteenth century. It still hung in the gallery.

'I hate London.' Nikolai looked at the unchanging prospect and said with feeling, 'Who'd be in a dirty, noisy city when they could be here?'

His grandfather smiled. 'I thought London was where everyone wanted to be these days,' he said mischievously. 'I suspect Véronique Repiquet would have preferred to have her wedding there. She told me London was cool.'

Nikolai raised his eyes to heaven. 'Véronique would! I, however, am thirty-six years old. I don't chase fads any more.'

'You seem to manage to have a pretty good time when you get there, however,' Pauli said drily.

Nikolai did not pretend to misunderstand him. 'Oops,' he said, wincing.

More than one celebrity-watch magazine had published photographs of Nikolai at last year's fashionable Christmas parties in London. He had been with a different woman in each picture, as his grandmother had pointed out acidly to her husband at the time. Pauli had just said it was nice to see that Nicki was getting over his brother's death and enjoying himself again.

He had tactfully not told his wife about the picture which had fallen out of one of Nikolai's Christmas cards last year. It had shown what looked like a student party in a cellar. The Countess would have been horrified by the sight of her grandson jamming at the piano, having discarded most of his clothes. Pauli, however, was more realistic, and even, as Nikolai knew, faintly envious.

'There must be friends you would like to look up,' Pauli pointed out now innocently. There had been a number of lively-looking girls in that picture.

Nikolai was dry. 'Which particular friend did you have in mind?'

But his grandfather shook his head. 'Matchmaking is your grandmother's department, not mine,' he said decisively. 'All I want is to make sure that Tatiana isn't being—er—unwise.'

'My great-aunt Tatiana,' said Nikolai, who had spent several strenuous hours with her and her accountant in December, and was not anxious to repeat the experience, 'is a self-willed old woman. She has been barking for years. I should think it is a cast-iron certainty that she is being unwise.'

Pauli did not bother to deny it. 'But you're fond of her,' he pointed out. 'You wouldn't want anyone to take advantage of her.'

Their eyes met in total mutual comprehension. Nikolai curbed his frustration.

'You should have been in public relations,' he said at last bitterly. 'Or politics. All right, Pauli. I'll go to London and check on Tatiana. What's the story?'

Lisa did not see much of Tatiana over the next few weeks. She was busy all day; and in the evenings, proving to herself as much as her old friends that she had not left them behind with her move, she went out clubbing.

Which was why, when the doorbell rang at ten o'clock on a Sunday morning, Lisa was still in bed.

'No,' she groaned. She pulled the pillow over her head, blocking both ears. 'Go away.'

But it rang again, insistently. Lisa gave up. Blearily she swung her legs out of bed and felt for a robe. Failing to find one, she pulled last night's coat round her instead.

As the bell rang for the third time she trod heavily up the stairs, muttering.

'What is it? Don't you know it's Sunday?' she growled as she flung the door open.

Nikolai Ivanov blinked. There was not much that shook him. He had a cool and generally well-justified confidence that there was nothing he had not seen before. But Lisa was a new phenomenon, even to a man of his experience.

He took an involuntary step backwards, his eyes widening in stunned silence. He would have said that he had seen all the weirder life forms, but he had never before encountered Lisa Romaine after a heavy night's clubbing. Getting back at five in the morning she had, quite literally, taken off her clothes and tumbled into bed. As a result her hair was still full of last night's rainbow colours, though some of the spikes had been flattened in sleep. She was also sporting panda shadows round her eyes from unstable mascara. To say nothing of her pugnacious expression.

Nikolai stared in appalled fascination. And found he could think of nothing to say.

'Well?' demanded Lisa.

The man on the doorstep was so tall it hurt her neck to look up at him. Squinting into the morning sun, Lisa made out high, haughty cheekbones and deep brown eyes under lazy lids. It was an arrogant face. And spectacularly handsome.

'What do you want?' she said, thoroughly put out.

Lisa did not like handsome men. She had learned the hard way that they tended to be more in love with themselves than any woman who happened to cross their path. It had soured her.

The handsome stranger scrutinised her for several unnerving seconds. It did nothing to mollify her.

'Who are you?' he demanded.

Lisa gave him an evil look.

'I'm the householder. I was fast asleep.'

He looked taken aback. Then, as if in spite of himself, he looked her up and down in one comprehensive survey. His mouth twitched.

'Now why doesn't that surprise me?' he murmured.

Lisa did not like being laughed at. She ran her hand through the residual spikes and glared.

'Either tell me what you want or go away.'

'Well, I did want to see the householder,' Nikolai admitted.

He should, of course, have demanded Tatiana immediately. But now the shock had worn off he found he was intrigued by this apparition. In her bare feet she came no higher than his chest. Yet she seemed quite unconscious of being at any sort of disadvantage. She might be half asleep, but she was still definitely punching her weight, he thought. He admired that.

Lisa folded her arms with exaggerated patience. It was a mistake because it made her coat gape. That revealed, if Nikolai had not already guessed it, that she was wearing nothing underneath.

He did not pretend that he hadn't noticed. His eyes widened and he stared openly. And if he did not actually laugh aloud, he did not try to disguise his amusement.

What he did disguise—at least Nikolai hoped so—was his sudden rush of pleasure at the sight. It was unexpected, unwelcome and deeply primitive. That intrigued him, too. He was in no rush to demand Tatiana until he had explored this feeling further.

Lisa seemed oblivious. 'You want to see me? You're seeing me,' she pointed out. 'So—?'

Nikolai let his eyes drift down. 'I am indeed,' he agreed, in suave appreciation.

Lisa was used to being teased. You did not survive in the dealing room if you let it bother you. Normally she ignored it. Now, after a quick look down, she clutched the coat together more securely over her breasts.

'What do you *want*?' she yelled, losing patience.

'I want to see the lady who owns this place,' he said more sharply.

Now that he'd had time to reflect on more than that distracting cleavage, Nikolai's amusement was abating abruptly. Where was Tatiana? Why did this gamine not mention her? Could it be that Pauli was right and his aunt had gone mad and signed over her home to some unknown waif off the street? Nikolai had been certain his grandfather was panicking unnecessarily. Now, for the first time, he wasn't sure.

Lisa saw the suspicion darken his eyes. It made him look like a tiger, watchful and dangerous. It contrasted oddly with his beautifully cut City suit. Somehow it just made him seem all the more powerful. And who the hell wore suits on a Sunday, anyway?

Then she remembered: Rob had warned her that Sam would make sure the bank checked up on the suitability of her new address. Surely he had just been winding her up? Surely it couldn't be true? But, with his suit and tie on a Sunday morning, what else did this man resemble but a banker at work? In fact, now she looked, she saw he even had a briefcase.

She said defiantly, 'I live here. Lisa Romaine, as it no doubt says in your dossier. Do you want a signature, or will you now go away and leave me in peace?'

The tiger's eyes narrowed to slits.

'And what has happened to Madame Lepatkina?'

Whatever Lisa had expected it was not that. In the act of closing the door, she hesitated.

'Tatiana?' she said, bewildered. How did her employers know about Tatiana?

'Well, at least you admit she exists,' the man said grimly.

He shouldered his way past her into the hall and shut the door behind him. In the narrow hall he seemed even taller. She wished she were wearing heels. Or shoes. Or *anything*. She huddled the coat round her.

Nikolai saw her sudden uncertainty and pressed home his advantage.

'Now, let's start again. Where is Tatiana?'

Lisa shrugged. Then remembered and grabbed the coat tight again.

'I haven't a clue. Why didn't you try knocking?'

He was disconcerted. 'There is only one bell,' he said, after a tiny pause.

'I know,' she said nastily. 'Mine. If you want to talk to Tatiana you use the knocker. Big black thing? Gargoyle's face? You can't miss it.'

She made to open the door on him again, but one look at him barring the way changed her mind. In spite of the suit he gave the impression of being solidly muscled. She frowned, swung round and thumped on Tatiana's door. There was no answer.

Lisa looked at her big Mickey Mouse watch. 'I suppose she might have gone shopping,' she said uncertainly.

'On a Sunday?'

She looked at him with dislike. 'This is cosmopolitan Notting Hill. You can shop any day you like.'

'And any *time* you like as well,' he pointed out. 'So why would Tatiana go shopping at the exact hour she knew I was coming to see her?'

Lisa seized the opportunity to look him up and down, in just the same way as he had done.

'You might just have answered your own question,' she drawled with deliberate insolence.

He was clearly disconcerted. Not used to people being less than delighted to see him, Lisa thought sourly. The thought rang a faint bell in her head.

She didn't have time to pursue it. The man was knocking at the door to Tatiana's part of the house. There was no answer. He looked back at Lisa, all the way down that haughty nose.

'Do you have a key to Tatiana's place?'

'No,' said Lisa.

His mouth tightened. He looked very determined. The inner bell rang louder.

She said grudgingly, 'I could go up through the garden and see if she's there.'

He nodded. 'Yes, that's an idea. All right.'

'"Thank you very much, Miss Romaine",' Lisa muttered.

He did not appear to hear.

Lisa thumped her way bad-temperedly down the stairs. She was sure nothing had happened to Tatiana. She had met her in the hall last night, off to attend a ballet recital, looking stupendously glamorous and about half her age. She had probably just gone out to avoid this pestilential stranger. What was more, Lisa didn't blame her.

She turned round to shout as much up to him, and found he was close on her heels.

'Oh,' she exclaimed, swaying backwards in shock.

He caught the lapels of her coat and steadied her.

And that was another shock. The backs of his fingers brushed against the softness of her upper breasts. It was only a touch, but it felt as if he had branded her. Lisa heard her own intake of breath. In the narrow space of the staircase it sounded as loud as a warning siren.

'Whoa,' she said, shaken.

Nikolai was shaken too. But his control was better than hers. And his recovery time was not affected by a series of late nights.

'Are you all right?' he said, his expression enigmatic.

'You startled me,' she muttered. 'I didn't expect you to come with me.'

'I could hardly leave you to climb into Tatiana's on your own.'

'Climb in?' said Lisa, startled.

'If necessary.'

She glared at him for a frustrated moment. Then shrugged and led the way downstairs.

Her small kitchen diner stretched the width of the house. Tall French windows gave on to the garden. Lisa waved a hand at them.

'Help yourself. Security key's on the table. I'll get some clothes on.'

He acknowledged that with the merest flicker of the opaque brown eyes. But Lisa could sense his amusement as if he had laughed out loud. Suddenly she realised what it must be like to blush. She whisked into her bedroom and closed the door between them with a decisive bang.

She returned in three minutes, in grubby jeans and a cropped shirt. She had stuffed her feet into deck shoes and tied a scarf round her hair, but she hadn't done anything about the ravages of last night's make-up. To tell the truth, Lisa had forgotten it. But to the man awaiting her it looked like a deliberate statement that she didn't care how he saw her.

Once again he felt that unexpected, unwanted kick of interest. Crazy, he told himself.

'Well?' said Lisa.

He had opened her French windows. An ironwork spiral staircase went up from the garden to Tatiana's balcony. There was a tray of seedlings and a watering can on the stair. He indicated them with a gesture.

'Well, if she's in the garden, of course she didn't hear us,' said Lisa, disgusted. She thought about what she had just said. She didn't like the way she had coupled them together like that. 'You,' she corrected herself. 'Of course she didn't hear you.' She raised her voice to the volume that could cut through the buzz of a hundred-man dealing room. 'Tatiana! Where are you?'

Nikolai winced. 'Wouldn't it be easier to go and look? It *is* Sunday morning, after all. Some people are probably still sleeping. Or—'

Or in bed making love. He did not say it. But Lisa's eyes flew to his in shocked and instant comprehension.

And this time she did blush. She couldn't help it. Disbelieving, she pressed her hands to her face and felt the heat there. She could never remember blushing in her life before.

And the man laughed. He looked her up and down with those cat's eyes, suddenly lazily appreciative, and he *laughed*.

'Oh, find her yourself,' snarled Lisa.

She whipped back into her flat and banged the door.

CHAPTER TWO

NIKOLAI cornered his aunt under a silver birch and came swiftly to the point.

'Who is she?'

Tatiana looked at her great-nephew in surprise. Nikolai could be very irritating. But he was usually much too laid-back to lose his temper in her experience. Now he was looking positively grim.

'You sound just like your Uncle Dmitri. In fact in that ridiculous suit you even look like him.'

They both knew it was not a compliment. Dmitri Ivanov was a merchant banker in New York. Tatiana thought Dmitri was a pompous ass and frequently said so at family reunions.

Nikolai waved the irrelevance aside impatiently.

'Who *is* she?'

Tatiana sighed and put down her trowel. She had been enjoying her gardening. 'Who is who?'

'The fierce person in the basement.'

In the middle of stripping off her gloves, Tatiana stopped, arrested. 'Lisa? My tenant Lisa? She's not fierce.'

Nikolai grimaced. 'She is if you get her out of bed before she's ready,' he said with feeling. 'She nearly bit my head off.'

'Oh?'

Tatiana stared into the middle distance, suddenly thoughtful.

'So where did she come from?'

'Mmm?'

'Lisa Whatever-her-name-is,' Nikolai said impatiently. 'Where did you find her?'

Tatiana remained distracted. 'Oh, around,' she said vaguely.

Nikolai curbed his irritation. Tatiana, he reminded himself, was old and eccentric, and probably worried about money.

So he said carefully, 'Why this sudden urge to become a landlady again?'

She shrugged. 'I've always let out rooms when I needed to.'

'But the point is,' said Nikolai patiently, 'you don't need to. I went through the figures last year and I saw your accountant again a couple of days ago. You don't need to do this. You can pay your way easily.'

Tatiana sniffed. Since she had given Pauli *carte blanche* to manage her affairs more than forty years ago, she could hardly claim that this was high-handed. But she could and did say that her decision was nothing to do with Nikolai.

'I like Lisa. I wanted her to have the flat.'

Nikolai looked at her narrowly. 'Is running the house getting too much for you?'

'No, of course not,' said Tatiana impatiently. 'I have a cleaner twice a week. What more do I need?'

'You are lonely, then?'

'I do too much to be lonely.'

'Then why—?'

Tatiana folded her lips together stubbornly. 'I told you. I like her. She needed somewhere to live and I—'

He pounced on it. '*Needed*. Aha. She is a vagrant. From what I saw this morning, I can well believe it.'

'Oh, Nicki, don't be pompous. Of course she's not a vagrant.'

'What do you know about her? Have you taken any references?'

'No, but—'

'I knew it. She is exploiting you.'

'Nikolai, will you listen to me? She has a perfectly good job.'

'Doing what?'

Tatiana had to admit she didn't know. She had simply not taken in what Lisa did for a living and had only the vaguest idea of where she worked.

Aware of this, she said defensively, 'I have known her for over a year. We go to the same dance studio.'

Nikolai was not stupid enough to look triumphant. But the faint hint of scepticism about his mouth infuriated Tatiana.

'And she is not exploiting me. In fact she's the one who has been insisting that we have a legal agreement.'

If anything, Nikolai's scepticism increased.

'Protecting her position,' he diagnosed. 'Very shrewd.'

'You know, it's very unhealthy, always thinking the worst of people. It gives you ulcers,' Tatiana informed him.

'So do great-aunts,' said Nikolai ruefully. He sobered. 'Now, are you going to ask her for references? Because if you don't I will.'

Tatiana looked infuriatingly ethereal. 'You must learn to trust more.'

'Right. I'll deal with it.'

He marched off without waiting for a reply. Tatiana did not permit herself to smile until there was no chance of his turning round and seeing it. But as soon as he was out of sight she threw her gloves up in the air and gave a whoop of triumph.

'*Yes!*'

Lisa heard the shout. By that time she had just about stopped dancing with rage. She had got to the point where she didn't know if she was angrier with herself for being so stupid, or Tatiana's visitor for being so arrogant.

Considering it, she realised that neither was the main course of her fury. It was the way he'd looked at her! Nobody looked at her like that. Nobody *dared*.

Angrily she stripped off her clothes and stamped into the bathroom. The floor-to-ceiling mirror showed her a slim figure, pale and shaking with temper—and a clown's mask of smudged paint.

Lisa was taken aback. She leaned towards the mirror, fingering the mascara experimentally. It spread.

If that was what he'd seen, maybe there was some excuse for the way he'd looked at her. It couldn't be often that the door was opened to a man like that by the Thing from the Black Lagoon. A brief laugh shook Lisa at the thought.

But then she took a firm grip of her anger again. Somehow she needed that anger; she didn't know why. Nobody had a right to look another person up and down as if they were a *thing*, she assured herself. Even if they were looking a little strange at the time. If she ever saw him again—which of course she did not want to—she would tell him so.

She stepped into the steaming shower and prepared to put him out of her mind.

Ten minutes later she was still polishing the scathing things she would never now have the opportunity of saying to him and surveying her fridge blankly. One packet of carrots, going mouldy. One carton of milk, rancid. Two bottles of mineral water. She needed coffee and she hated it black. So—

A glance out of the French windows she had locked in the hateful man's face told Lisa that it was raining. It looked cold, too. She really did not want to go out. But her stomach rumbled threateningly.

Quiet, she told it. Black coffee won't hurt you for once. I'll give the man time to go and then I'll borrow some milk from Tatiana.

She sat down to wait. But the morning stretched into lunchtime, and there was no sound of the front door closing behind him. Lisa looked at the rain, now falling in a sheet.

'Damn,' she said.

She fetched an umbrella.

Nikolai was angry. He was sitting in his hired car, watching his aunt's house like a private eye. It felt seedy and faintly ludicrous. He didn't like either sensation.

Something else that was the fault of the downstairs tenant, he thought. On top of defying him, and then making him feel as if he was holding onto his control by the thinnest of threads! It was intolerable. It had to be put right. He had told Tatiana that he would deal with it. So he would.

He didn't have to wait long. The front door opened and a figure huddled under an umbrella scurried out. She could not have looked more furtive if she was running away from the police, thought Nikolai. It filled him with an obscure triumph.

Lisa didn't notice the man sitting in the Lexus across the road. She hurried along, head bent. The wind blew the rain in little swirls against which the umbrella was almost no use at all. In the end she put it in front of her like a battering ram, and, looking neither to right nor left, she pelted for the shop.

Nikolai put the car in gear and slid it smoothly out of its tight parking place. Lisa didn't notice that either, deep in her absorption.

If only the horrible man hadn't woken her up, she thought, she could still be fast asleep, without this need for milky coffee and a bun. And she wouldn't be feeling the sting of having made a complete idiot of herself. And the weather made everything ten times worse.

She dived into the small supermarket and emerged with an unwieldy bag containing the Sunday papers, a litre of milk, a crusty baguette that she did not want but hadn't been able to resist the smell of, and a pineapple—luxurious but low on calories. In fact the smell of new bread had cheered her up so much that it put a bounce in her step. She swung out of the door so energetically that she bumped into some-one.

'Oh, I'm sorry—' she began, genuinely contrite. And then saw who it was.

Her smile died. 'What are you doing here?'

Nikolai did not pretend. 'Following you.'

'Following—' Even though it was what she'd suspected, Lisa was lost for words.

'I wanted to talk to you,' he said, as if that was justification enough.

'You've talked,' Lisa said shortly.

Her carrier bag began to tip. Nikolai caught the wavering baguette.

'Rather too aerodynamic, these things, aren't they?' he said pleasantly enough.

Then, to Lisa's outraged astonishment, he broke the end of the crust off and ate it.

'Not bad,' he said, with the air of a connoisseur.

Lisa clutched her purchases to her breast before he could pillage any more.

'And you're an expert, I suppose?' she said scathingly.

Nikolai gave her a wicked grin. 'Pretty practised, yes.'

The grin was alarmingly attractive. It set off all sorts of warning bells in Lisa's head. She didn't want to be attracted to any man. In her experience it was a distraction at best, at worst a one way ticket to misery. And this man was arrogant and had already made her feel as much a fool as she had done in years.

So she hugged her lumpy package protectively and jerked her head in the direction of the shop's interior.

'Well, they're on sale in there. Help yourself.'

She made to pass him. Nikolai did not move.

'I told you. I want to talk to you.'

'Great,' said Lisa bristling. 'Does it matter what *I* want?'

'I'm afraid not,' he said. He didn't sound in the least apologetic.

He hoisted the carrier out of her arms.

'Come along. I have a car and we're getting wet.'

Lisa stood stock-still. 'Give me back my shopping,' she said in a dangerously quiet voice.

'Don't be difficult,' Nikolai said with odious patience.

Still quietly, Lisa said, 'Then don't challenge me.'

She held out her hand for the bag. He held onto it.

'You have to admit you'd be more comfortable in my car. We'll talk and then I'll drive you home.'

Her expression was very steady. Too steady, her colleagues would have told him. Nikolai did not recognise the danger signals.

'I don't do what I'm told,' she said. 'And I warn you, I fight dirty.'

'Who's fighting? Nikolai said softly.

He gave her his most charming smile. The one that made hostesses forgive him for arriving late and had girls lure him home for coffee after an evening together. On Lisa it had no effect at all.

She stood looking at him for an appraising moment. Then she put her head back and screamed at the top of powerful lungs. It startled Nikolai so much that he dropped the unwieldy bag. And it brought an interested audience out onto the pavement to join them.

Lisa stopped screaming. She gathered up the shopping.

'Thank you,' she said composedly.

She turned her back and walked away from him. It felt good. So good, in fact, that she didn't bother to put up the umbrella. Instead she lifted her face to the rain and let it cascade off her cold skin. She even broke into a little run of pleasure.

She was halfway home when the powerful car caught up with her. It cruised to a halt on the wrong side of the road, beside a line of parked cars. Nikolai opened the window and called across to her.

'Round one to you,' he said. 'I still need to talk to you.'

Lisa sent him a look of dislike. She steamed on, not saying anything. The shopping bag bumped against her legs. The baguette had snapped, of course. It hung over the edge of the bag at a crazy angle, smeared with dirt from where it had hit the wet pavement.

Nikolai called after her temptingly, 'I've got you a replacement loaf.'

Lisa ignored him.

He kept the car cruising in second gear, matching her pace. Lisa looked at him with irritation.

'In this country we drive on the left.'

Nikolai chuckled. 'In London, you drive where you can get through. Anyone will be able to pass me,' he said with confidence. 'But if you got in the car I could go back to driving on the legal side of the road.'

She shrugged, still marching. 'Break the law if you like. I don't care.'

'That's not a very responsible attitude,' said Nikolai reprovingly. He was beginning to enjoy himself.

Lisa fixed her eyes straight ahead. 'I'm not responsible for anyone but myself. You want to behave like a nutter—your choice.'

'It's raining. The car is warm and dry,' he said temptingly.

Lisa did not abate her pace. 'My mother always told me never to get into cars with strange men.'

'But, as we have already established, you are more than able to take care of yourself,' Nikolai said ruefully. 'Besides, I'm not a stranger. I'm Tatiana's nephew.'

That brought Lisa up short. She did stop then. In disbelief, she turned to face the car. Nikolai brought it gently to a halt and sat returning her stare.

'The jungle warrior?'

Suddenly Nikolai was not enjoying himself quite so much. A faint look of annoyance crossed the handsome face.

'I do go on expeditions to the jungle, yes.'

'Beard?' said Lisa gropingly. 'Camouflage trousers?'

'Not in London,' said Nikolai stiffly.

The annoyance turned to downright affront. The terrible girl had started to laugh.

It was not a quiet laugh. She flung back her head and let out a full-throated peal of delight. To a wincing Nikolai, the sound seemed to bounce between the Palladian terraces with the resonance of a kettle drum.

'Are you always this noisy?' he said, irritated.

'Yup,' said Lisa without apology.

Nikolai looked at her with frustration. It had started to rain heavily again. He set the windscreen wipers going.

Now that the rainbow spikes had gone, he saw that she was a blonde. The rain was plastering her hair to her head. Her head, he noticed with a little shock of pleasure, was a very elegant shape.

He had not thought of elegance in relation to this girl before. She had called herself a dirty fighter, and a street fighter was exactly how she had looked when she'd opened the door this morning. Now, suddenly, he was seeing deeper: long throat, porcelain skin, deep-set wide open eyes with gently curling lashes. Her eyelashes, he saw with an odd clutch in his stomach, were long enough for the rain-drops to gather on. He wanted to lift the drops off with his fingertip.

It startled him. It also made him angry. This was not a girl he wanted to be attracted to. She was too rude and too loud and he had severe doubts about the honesty of her dealings with his aunt. Yet here he was, thinking about her as if he wanted to take her to bed. He was furious with himself. It translated into fury with her.

'Get in,' he said. It was an order.

Lisa jumped. Her laughter died. She raised her chin belligerently.

'Don't tell me what to do,' she flashed.

But Nikolai had had enough. 'Then stop playing games. You're no helpless innocent. And you don't think I'm any threat to you. For God's sake be sensible and get out of the rain.'

Slightly to her own surprise, Lisa did.

Nikolai set the car in motion. 'Now,' he said. 'Let's start again. Who are you?'

Having surrendered a point by getting into the expensive comfort of his car, Lisa was going to make him fight for every scrap of information he got out of her.

'What's it got to do with you?'

Nikolai looked at her out of the corner of his eye. 'Tatiana,' he said quietly, 'is my great-aunt. We don't see enough of her but that doesn't mean we forget her. Besides, I am very fond of her.'

'Oh.' Lisa bit her lip. She was fond of Tatiana too. To her regret, she had to admit that he had a point.

Nikolai hid a triumphant smile.

'So, who are you and where do you come from?' His tone was quite pleasant but it demanded an answer.

Lisa shrugged and gave him one.

'Lisa Romaine. Tatiana and I go to the same dance studio.'

'So she said. And that's not quite what I meant,' said Nikolai drily.

A faint flicker of resentment returned. 'What do you want to know?' she snapped. 'My ancestry for the last six generations and my bra size?'

He was taken aback.

'I think we can skip the ancestry,' he said smoothly. 'I was thinking along the lines of where you lived before and whether you work.'

Lisa was insulted. 'Of course I work. I'm Head of Bond Trading at Napier Kraus.'

The car slewed dangerously close to the parked cars. Nikolai braked.

'Napier Kraus?' He saw enough of Uncle Dmitri at family gatherings to know the bank's name—and know that it was not a lightweight institution. 'You're a banker?' he said blankly.

Lisa was pleased with the reaction. 'I told you. A bond trader.'

'You don't look like a banker,' said Nikolai, unheeding. There was a strong note of indignation in his voice.

'Oh?' said Lisa dangerously.

He didn't notice the danger. 'You're too young. Too scruffy. Too—'

'Female?'

He did hear it then. For a moment his face went blank. Then he glanced sideways at her and drawled very deliberately, 'Well, you're certainly not feminine.'

There was a sharp silence. Then Lisa gave a silent whistle.

'Oh, very nasty,' she congratulated him in her most affable tone. 'You must be a real barrel of laughs in the jungle.'

Nikolai was annoyed with himself. 'I just thought—'

'Yes?' She was too angry to let him off the hook. 'I'd be interested to know just exactly what you *did* think.'

That was when Nikolai made a tactical error. 'Tatiana knows some strange people. And she can be—unwary.'

There was a long pause.

Then Lisa said on a note of discovery, 'You think I'm a con artist.'

He did not deny it.

Lisa began to shake, very slightly.

It had happened before, but not very often. Usually when someone threatened her family; once or twice when it had been Lisa herself in a corner and fighting for the job on which they all depended. It had something to do with survival and a lot more to do with justice.

Now the unfairness of it blinded her. For a glorious moment she lost control of her temper and let it ride her. Straight to the devil, if that was where it wanted to go.

She said sweetly, viciously, 'After all, a scruff like me couldn't rent a room in a posh place like this any other way, could she?'

Nikolai was taken aback. He hadn't expected retaliation so swift or to the point.

'I shouldn't have said that you were scruffy,' he said stiffly. 'I apologise.'

'Oh, why bother?' She gave him a glittering smile. 'It's so much easier to do business if you're straight with each other, don't you think?'

At once he was very still. 'Are we going to do business, then?'

Lisa widened her green eyes and gave him her sweetest smile. 'Aren't we?' she asked dulcetly.

She was so angry she could barely hold it together. But she was not going to let him see that. Instead she was going to lead him to think that she was the worst sort of con artist he could imagine—and then show him there was not a thing he could do about it. It was time somebody showed this control freak that he was no master of the universe.

They were back in Stanley Crescent now. There was the tightest possible parking space on the opposite side of the road from Tatiana's house. Lisa, who did not like driving, thought he would never slot the car into it. She fell silent, in pleased anticipation.

But to her annoyance Nikolai backed in at first go. He hardly seemed to notice the difficult manoeuvre at all. He was frowning, but not about wheel angles.

'Are you asking me to pay you to leave my aunt's house?' he said bluntly.

Lisa inspected her nails.

Nikolai said softly, 'Let me warn you now. I'm not a good subject for blackmail.'

'And I'm not a good subject for bullying.' She gave him a bland smile and unlocked her seat belt. 'Should make for an interesting negotiation.'

'I am not,' said Nikolai between his teeth, 'going to negotiate with a woman like you.'

Lisa could feel the rage in him. And the frustration. It gave her a heady sense of power that almost swamped the effect of the insult. Almost.

'Up to you,' she said, and reached for her shopping.

His hand closed over her arm. For a moment Lisa blinked in real alarm. He was shockingly strong. Suddenly she could believe in his jungle prowess. Quickly she reminded herself that she was not afraid of him. She even gave a scornful laugh.

Their eyes met. Lisa's expression dared him. Nikolai's grip relaxed a fraction. But he did not let her go.

'Don't even think about it,' he said.

'About what?'

'Taking me on.' He let her go and drew back, considering her with a connoisseur's deliberation. 'You can't win, you know.'

'I can do anything I choose,' Lisa said calmly. 'I have something you want and we both know it.'

The atmosphere in the car was suddenly arctic.

'Oh?' Nikolai sounded mildly interested, but Lisa knew he was wound up tight as a spring. 'And what do you think that is?'

She showed her teeth.

'Squatters' rights.'

Lisa swung out of the car. Nikolai didn't move to prevent her. He was sitting very still, his expression frozen.

At last Lisa gave vent to her fury, if only for a moment. She slammed the car door with the full force of her arm. Nikolai winced.

She crossed the street without looking back.

Nikolai picked up the car phone and dialled.

'Hi, Tom,' he said when it was answered. 'I'm going to have to take a raincheck on lunch. Something's come up.'

'And Sedgewick? What do I do with him? *I'm* not the one who wants to go with him to Borneo.'

'Hang onto him. I'll be over later.'

Tom was not best pleased. 'He goes at teatime, whether you've caught her by then or not,' said Tom firmly.

Nikolai grinned for the first time in what seemed like hours.

'Caught her? I don't know what you mean.'

Tom ignored that. 'How long have I known you, Nicki? Put the skirt on ice for the afternoon. If you really want to go on this expedition.'

Nikolai was injured. 'You've got a suspicious mind. I am dealing with my great-aunt's affairs.'

'Affairs, I believe,' Tom said drily. 'Four o'clock, latest. Or forget Borneo.' He hung up.

Nikolai got out of the car.

As soon as Lisa let herself in to the house she saw that Tatiana's door was now open. Immediately Tatiana herself appeared, almost as if she was waiting for her.

'Are you all right?' the older woman asked.

'Of course I'm all right,' said Lisa furiously. 'Did you think your nephew would bombard me with poison darts?'

Tatiana blinked. She hadn't seen Lisa in a temper before.

'He—er—said you'd met.'

'Met! Well, you could call it that, I suppose.'

Tatiana began to be alarmed. 'What did he do?'

'To be precise,' said Lisa, 'he leered down my cleavage. Then he accused me of fraud.'

She was still shaking. Tatiana saw it.

'Oh, dear,' she said. 'He has upset you.'

'He could not,' said Lisa with precision, 'upset me if he tried. All men are a joke. And your nephew is a caveman and a bigot as well.'

She clattered downstairs, dashing away angry tears. Going straight to the bathroom, she splashed cold water on her hot face. Her reflection in the mirror looked like an angry cat.

Lisa's temper subsided somewhat. She leaned forward and rested her hot forehead against the glass. She sighed.

Men! It was enough to make a woman weep. They caused so much trouble: Sam hating to admit that she was good at her job and doing everything he could to denigrate her; Alec deciding he was in love with her so that she had to move out; the whole dreary succession of men over whom her sister Kit had broken first her heart and then her health. Lisa's mother, Joanne, watched her daughter like a hawk, but Kit seemed to have an unerring instinct for finding men

who would use her badly and leave her flat. And then she
punished herself because they didn't love her. Lisa's eyes
pricked with unexpected tears again as she remembered.

And now Nikolai Ivanov, King of the Jungle, accused her
of trying to blackmail him! Lisa ground her teeth, reviving
at the thought. Well, if he wanted a fight, she was going to
show him that she was every bit as tough and nasty as he
thought she was. And she was going to *win*.

The doorbell rang. Lisa had no doubt at all who it was.
She whipped upstairs, past Tatiana in her doorway, and
flung it open like a cavalry charge.

'*Go away!*'

Unseen behind her, Tatiana bit back a smile and retreated
into her own part of the house. Neither Lisa nor Nikolai
noticed.

He held out the shopping she had left in his car and stood
his ground.

'We started off on the wrong foot,' he said. 'My fault.
I'm really sorry. Can we start again?'

Lisa was unimpressed. 'Is this the charm offensive now?'

A faint look of annoyance crossed the handsome face.

And it was handsome, Lisa had to admit. He had deep-
set eyes over high cheekbones and a thin, haughty nose.
And his mouth! In the days before she had decided men
were a waste of space Lisa had been rather a connoisseur
of mouths. And in this one, wide and mobile, she read sen-
suality warring with control. Which would win if it came to
all-out war? she pondered. It would be a challenge to find
out.

Lisa came to herself with a start. Would have been a
challenge, she corrected herself. Would have been. In the
past. In the days when she had still been playing games like
that. Now the whole idea left her unmoved. Didn't it?

Nikolai curbed his annoyance and permitted himself to
look penitent.

'I was unfair,' he said mendaciously. 'Put it down to my

affection for Tatiana. Let me make amends. Why don't I buy you a late lunch?'

Lisa gaped.

His smile deepened the lights in his eyes until they looked as warm as a friendly fire on a dark night. It was the sort of smile a lot of girls would dream about turning to…drowning in… Fortunately she was not one of them, Lisa reminded herself.

'Why?' she croaked.

'You can tell me all about your arrangement with my aunt Tatiana. And I'll tell you anything you want to know about me.'

She toyed with the idea of saying she didn't want to know a thing about him. Then she saw his expression. That was exactly what he was expecting her to say. Lisa stopped herself just in time.

'A name would be nice,' she said drily.

And saw with real triumph the way the phoney warmth flickered out.

Nikolai recovered quickly. 'I'm sorry. Nikolai Ivanov.'

He held out a hand. To her own annoyance, Lisa found herself shaking it. His fingers were long and she had that tingling sensation of his physical strength again. She pulled her hand away.

'Hello and goodbye,' she said curtly.

'I told you, we need to get better acquainted,' he drawled, amused. 'Come on, have a meal with me. Call it compensation for waking you up.' Nikolai's voice was soft, but he sounded horribly determined.

Lisa felt a shiver of reaction. She hung onto her cool irreverence. But it was an effort. 'No need.'

'Oh, but there is.' He smiled straight into her eyes. 'If you don't come, we'll both die of—shall we call it curiosity?'

Lisa could hear the blood pounding in her ears. How did he *do* that? She swallowed.

Hardly believing it, she heard herself say, 'All right. Let me unload the groceries and you can take me to 192.'

Nikolai nodded, without comment.

She wasn't sure whether that indicated that he knew the fashionable local brasserie or that he accepted her acquiescence. Probably the latter, thought Lisa, annoyed with herself. To judge by his expression it was only what he'd expected.

She hugged the carrier bag to her and ran downstairs. Nikolai followed. Quickly she unloaded the groceries while he strolled around the sitting room. She braced herself to parry a cutting comment but he said nothing. Balked, she disappeared into the bedroom to change.

When she came back he was sitting in a bamboo chair that was one of the few pieces of her own furniture in the room, putting down the phone.

'What are you doing?' Lisa demanded, instantly suspicious.

'Booking a table.'

He had stood up when she came in. Now he surveyed her appreciatively. Lisa had changed into slim black trousers and a leather jacket over a peacock silk shirt. The silk, Nikolai was prepared to admit, was a welcome surprise.

'Nice,' he said.

Lisa's chin tilted to a challenging angle.

He didn't rise to it. 'Let's go.'

He did not make the mistake of taking her arm, but when they got to the car he opened the passenger door for her courteously. Lisa looked incredulous. Clearly not used to being treated like a lady, Nikolai thought. He bit back a smile and held the door a little wider.

Lisa laughed. Her eyes crinkled up at the corners when she laughed. It made her look like a mischievous little animal, Nikolai thought. She ran on the spot, shaking the rain out of her eyes.

'You aren't seriously thinking of *driving* there? Great heavens, it's ten minutes' walk, tops.'

It was Nikolai's turn to stare. When he took girls out, he was used to taking them right to the door of the restaurant. They expected it. Especially in London's weather.

'But it's raining.'

Lisa shook her head scornfully. 'You know, no one would think you were a great explorer,' she informed him.

For a moment, Nikolai's sense of humour got the better of him.

'I'm very sorry,' he murmured. 'Shall I throw you over my shoulder and swing from lamp post to lamp post?'

Lisa gave a choke of startled laughter. 'I'd like to see you try.'

His eyes gleamed. He took a step towards her. But Lisa was already off down the street.

'Come on,' she called. 'I'm hungry and I'm getting wet.'

Nikolai laughed and followed her.

The restaurant was exactly as he remembered it from December: gleaming with chrome and minimalist furniture and full of delectable smells. It was too late for it to be full but several people were still perched at the bar reading the restaurant's lavish supply of Sunday newspapers.

Lisa looked round with pleasure. 'I like this place. Nobody shows off.'

Nikolai surveyed a rumpled redhead, alternating wine and black coffee at the bar. The face was famous. The casual clothes bore designer labels and it looked as if she had slept in them. He gave a soft laugh.

'I see what you mean.'

A friendly woman, more elegant than any of her current customers, seated them and gave them menus. Nikolai saw with amusement that Lisa didn't bother to glance at hers.

'Come here often?' he asked blandly.

Lisa took a policy decision. Her feelings about this man were not going to spoil her lunch. She was starving and she knew the food here was heavenly.

So she grinned and told him the truth. 'Well, I don't cook.'

Nikolai was curious. 'I don't know many women who would admit that,' he remarked. 'Why not?'

Lisa chuckled. 'That sounds dangerously sexist.'

'Does it?' He didn't care, and it showed. 'Don't you like cooking?'

She shrugged, her amusement dying. 'Never learned,' she said briefly.

A waitress arrived. Lisa gave her order without waiting for Nikolai to ask her. His eyebrows rose involuntarily.

She saw it and stuck out her chin again. 'Yes?'

'Nothing.' He gave his own order. 'And what would you like to drink? Bucks Fizz? Kir Royale? Something else?'

'Oh, Bucks Fizz,' said Lisa impatiently, as uninterested as if she drank champagne every day.

He nodded to the waitress, who wrote it down, gathered up the menus and left.

Before she was out of earshot Lisa was demanding, 'Why did you look at me like that?'

'Like what?' said Nikolai, prevaricating.

'Like I'd just spat gum into the sugar bowl.'

He blinked. 'What a horrible idea.'

'Quite,' said Lisa drily. 'So what did I do?'

'Nothing of any importance,' said Nikolai smoothly. 'Now tell me, how did you meet Tatiana?'

But Lisa was not going to let him off the hook. 'What did I do?'

He made a deprecating gesture. 'I wouldn't want to offend you.'

'Force yourself,' said Lisa hardily. 'I want to know.'

'But it is not important,' he said. There was a slight edge to the suave voice now.

She leaned forward. 'You might as well tell me. I'm not going to shut up until you do.'

Nikolai lost his suavity altogether. He looked at her in some dudgeon. 'You must be a very difficult girlfriend.'

Lisa sat back in her seat and gave him a dangerous smile.

'That's not something you have to worry about, is it?' she said sweetly. 'Tell.'

He shrugged, and did.

There was a small, incredulous silence.

'I ought to have waited for you to ask me what I wanted to eat?' Lisa said at last. She sounded stunned.

Nikolai gave her a forgiving smile. 'As I am your host, it would have been polite. A small convention. As I said, it is not important.'

Lisa shook her head. 'It's barmy.'

Nikolai stiffened. If she had been apologetic, he would have assured her that it was nothing. He would even have meant it. Faced with outright revolt, however, he felt he had something to defend.

'On the contrary, it's civilised.'

Lisa made a rude noise.

Nikolai gave her a narrow-eyed smile. 'There are some benefits to civilisation, you know,' he drawled. 'I spend my working life studying animal behaviour, so I know what I'm talking about.' It was a challenge and they both knew it.

Lisa's head reared up. 'Are you calling me an animal?'

'We are all animals. Some of us just learn to curb our grosser instincts.'

Lisa drew a shaken breath. 'You don't pull your punches, do you?'

Nikolai raised his eyebrows. 'Do you?'

Their eyes met with the force of a lightning strike. Lisa blinked.

Then she shook her head. 'No,' she said slowly. 'No, I suppose I don't.'

'Something we have in common, then,' he said with pleasure.

'We have *nothing* in common,' Lisa said positively.

She was tempted to walk out, but the waitress came back with their drinks. Somehow it seemed silly to make a scene with the waitress as audience. It was not as if they were arguing lovers, for heaven's sake.

So she sat tight and took a long swig of the orange concoction.

Making her voice deliberately brisk, she said, 'Now look, Boris—'

He frowned. 'Nikolai.'

Lisa waved a careless hand. 'Whatever. I'm hungry and arguing is bad for the digestion. So let's get it over with. What do you want to know?'

Nikolai gave her a slow, caressing smile. It was one that usually worked like a dream. On Lisa, however, it had no detectable effect. She raised her eyebrows, scepticism written all over her.

Nikolai was piqued. He did not let it show, however.

'What does any man want to know about an attractive woman?' he said easily.

Lisa was not deceived. 'Oh, please.'

He abandoned the caressing manner with a shrug.

'OK. Have it your own way.' He leaned forward. 'Tell me everything there is to know.'

And he smiled into her eyes with deliberate intimacy. Anyone watching would have been fully justified in thinking they were lovers. For a crazy moment, Lisa almost thought it herself.

She clung to sanity in a reeling world. 'You *do* want my ancestry and my bra size,' she said astringently, dragging her eyes away.

His smile widened. 'If that's where you want to start,' he said smoothly.

Lisa thrust her hands into the pockets of her leather jacket and unobtrusively clutched it across her breast.

'I've been with Napier Kraus since I was sixteen. Dealing room all the time. Now, as I said, I'm Head of Bond Trading,' she said crisply.

Nikolai nodded, as if he were committing it to memory. 'Family?'

She was surprised. 'I have a mother and a sister. End of family.'

There was something in her voice which made him narrow his eyes. 'Close?'

'We keep in touch,' said Lisa evasively.

'Does Tatiana know them?'

'Why should she?'

He was frowning. 'So you met at dance class. You talked—' He looked up with a shrewd expression. 'What did you talk about?'

'Life,' she said flippantly.

'Yours or hers?'

She sighed. 'Both, as a matter of fact. It's called communication.'

Nikolai smiled triumphantly. 'So how come she doesn't know where you work or what you do?'

'Because she's not interested.' Lisa nearly shouted it. 'Don't you know your great-aunt at all? I work in the City. With money. She doesn't talk about money. Sex, yes. Even death, sometimes. Not money. It's vulgar and men deal with it. That's Tatiana's philosophy.'

Nikolai watched her with an arrested expression. At length he said, 'She is at least two generations ahead of you. It's not surprising she should see things differently.'

Lisa took a swallow of her drink and then turned the glass round and round in her hands, looking at the golden depths as if she was seeing something very different. Suddenly she was not indignant any more.

'I don't think that's just a generation difference,' she said at last, quietly. 'People on the edge of survival have always talked about money, I think.'

He sat as still as he knew how. As still as he had sat in the Goreng Forest, watching reintroduced gorillas reclaim their birthright. As still as he had sat in the Anderson Gorge, listening for the tell-tale fall of pebbles that signalled the start of an avalanche.

Around them the cheerful noise of a popular restaurant rose and fell. But Nikolai Ivanov concentrated all his attention on the silent woman opposite. And she did not notice.

At last he stirred.

'What do you know about the edge of survival?'

It was so casual it seemed as if it were just idle conversation. You would have said that he really didn't care one way or the other. But his eyes weren't casual. And Lisa was too distracted by memories to notice.

'When did you...' he paused, changed what he was going to say '...start working for Napier Kraus?'

Lisa looked up, her eyes still far away. Not a very happy place, he thought.

'I told you, straight from school,' she said without much interest. She gave herself a mental shake and returned to the fray. 'Does that answer all your questions?'

'Hardly.' He surveyed her for a frowning moment. 'How much have you told Tatiana?'

Lisa looked at him with a contempt she didn't even try to hide.

'She didn't ask the same questions as you.'

'What did she ask?'

'Well, she knows I don't come from what you would call a "good family",' Lisa said with bite.

Nikolai was annoyed. 'That's not what I asked.'

'Isn't it?'

Their food arrived. She picked up her knife and fork and attacked a cutlet as if it was a personal enemy. One she had to finish off *fast*.

Nikolai watched for a moment. Then he said, with that edge back in his voice, 'If you're trying to prove to me what a little savage you are, don't bother. I'm convinced.'

Another man had called her that. Lisa thought she had forgotten, but the word brought all the hairs up on the back of her neck. She felt winded. Her eyes flashed.

Nikolai gave a reluctant laugh.

'One *hell* of a girlfriend,' he said with feeling. 'How do the men in your life handle it?'

Lisa's eyes narrowed to slits. '*He,*' she said, deliberately misleading, 'survives.'

Nikolai made a great show of surprise. 'Only one?'

'One at a time, anyway.'

'An old-fashioned girl,' he mocked.

'An old-fashioned *savage*,' she corrected with venom.

He had the grace to look ashamed. 'That was uncalled for. I'm sorry.'

'Don't be. I don't care what you think of me.'

'I can see that.' He paused. 'And does this fortunate man also live in Tatiana's basement?'

Lisa looked at her cutlets. 'I think that's my business.'

'And Tatiana is mine,' Nikolai said with a hint of sharpness. He leaned forward, trying to force her to meet his eyes. 'She is elderly and alone. In some ways she is very unworldly. It's up to me to see that she isn't exploited. What would you do in my place?'

She looked up. 'Why are you so suspicious of me?'

'According to Tatiana, she virtually took you in off the street. Yet you claim to have a job everyone knows pays a fortune. Wouldn't you be suspicious in my place?'

There was something in what he said. But Lisa disliked him too much to admit it, even to herself.

'Oh, would you like a copy of my bank statement as well?' Her voice dripped sarcasm. 'Or—no. Bank statement *and* wage-slip, of course.'

'Don't be silly,' he said sharply. 'And I'm suspicious because I know that bond dealers are licensed to gamble bigtime and get paid a proportion of their winnings. Now, either you're not very good—in which case you must be lying when you say Napier Kraus has made you head of the department—or you can afford to buy a luxury penthouse somewhere. Living in Tatiana's basement just doesn't fit.'

Lisa tensed. But all she said was, 'If Tatiana isn't worried, I don't see what it has to do with you.'

'The fact that Tatiana isn't worried is exactly my problem.'

She shrugged. 'I don't think Tatiana is as gullible as you seem to think. She's an independent woman. She still has a damned good career. She doesn't need you to look after her.'

Nikolai surveyed her unspeaking for a moment. 'You mean you would *prefer* she had no one to look after her.'

'That is so patronising—' Lisa exploded.

'Oh, very good,' he applauded. 'Call the concerned relative a chauvinist pig and he'll slink away, apologising. Well, I'm not given to apologising. And I do what's necessary, whether other people like it or not. Especially when they're manipulative con artists with a good line in political correctness.' He was very angry.

Lisa looked at her cutlets. She had hardly touched them. But another mouthful would choke her. She put down her knife and fork and pushed her plate away.

'Then there's no point in continuing this.' She gathered up her tiny handbag. 'Thank you for lunch.' She didn't sound in the least grateful.

Nikolai sighed elaborately and leaned back in his chair. 'What on earth has come over Tatiana? Do you know?'

Lisa's head reared up. 'Maybe she just likes me.'

'That's exactly what I mean,' he drawled.

'Haven't you ever just liked someone?' she flashed.

'Not to the extent of letting them move in with me.'

Lisa's lip curled. 'I can well believe it.' She stood up. 'Well, you don't like me and I certainly don't want to spend any more time on this.' She fished in her handbag and brought out a small white oblong. She tossed it down on the table. 'My business card,' she said curtly. 'Do whatever checking up you want. Just don't come near me again.'

And before Nikolai could say another word, or even get to his feet, she walked out.

CHAPTER THREE

NIKOLAI got to Tom's before lunch had ended. Tom welcomed him into their tiny flat while his girlfriend, Melissa, pressed a bowl of assorted desserts into Nikolai's hand and cleared a place for him next to the great expedition leader.

'Ivanov,' said Professor Sedgewick through a mighty mouthful of bread and butter pudding. He swallowed hard, rose, shook hands with enthusiasm and sank back down again in one jerky movement. 'My dear chap, what a pleasure at last. Meant to write and tell you how much I admired your work on the Macaques. But things go out of my head unless my wife is there to remind me.'

'Well, she must have done,' said Nikolai, entertained. 'You sent me a very nice letter. My publishers cannibalised the best bits for the dustjacket, I'm afraid.'

'Good, good,' said the professor, with the vagueness of one whose publishers never told him what they were doing to publicise his books in case he torpedoed it. 'Now, you're going to come to Borneo with me, is that right?'

Nikolai was taken aback by this forthright approach.

'I'd be very flattered, of course, but...'

'Other commitments?' The professor was sympathetic. 'Book deadlines? Blasted television companies?' His tone filled with loathing. 'Graduate students?'

'No, nothing like that. The commitments are personal, I'm afraid.'

The professor looked bewildered for a moment. Then brightened.

'Bring her with you. Lovely place for a honeymoon, Borneo.'

Melissa made a choking sound. Tom stared her down.

'That's a very good thought,' said Nikolai, with only the faintest quiver of amusement in his voice. 'But I'm not getting married. To be honest, the commitment is to my grandparents.'

This was clearly beyond the professor entirely. So he ignored it, talking about the expedition to return wild orangutan to the Borneo jungle as if Nikolai's membership of the party was a foregone conclusion.

When he finally left, Tom clapped Nikolai on the shoulder.

'Jungle in October for you, then, you jammy devil. Sedgewick's all the more interested because you didn't seem too keen.' He cocked an eyebrow. 'Are you being Machiavellian, or might something really stop you going?'

Nikolai hesitated.

'Don't be nosy, Tom,' protested Melissa.

Tom laughed, unabashed. 'The skirt?'

'No,' said Nikolai, with more violence than the denial really required.

Tom's eyebrows flew up in comic surprise.

Nikolai added more moderately, 'It's my grandparents. Or the estate, to be more precise. I've been helping to run it since my brother died.'

Tom sobered. He had known Nikolai a long time and stayed with him in the horrible aftermath of Vladimir Ivanov's death in a car accident. He knew the burden of responsibility that Nikolai carried as the last surviving grandson.

'That was over a year ago,' he protested more quietly. 'Your grandparents can't expect you to put your career on hold for ever.'

Nikolai's expression was unencouraging. 'They don't.'

'Well, then—'

'I'll think about it,' Nikolai said with finality.

And, knowing him, Tom recognised that the subject was closed.

'So, who's the new girlfriend?' he said, slipping smoothly into a different gear.

Nikolai looked irritated. 'She's no girlfriend of mine, thank God.'

'Yet you very nearly stood up Sedgewick and Borneo for her,' teased Tom. 'She's got to have something.'

'Oh, she has indeed.' In retrospect Nikolai was not at all pleased with the way he had handled Lisa Romaine. It showed in his voice when he said, 'The woman has moved in on an elderly aunt of mine. Obviously she sold her some sob story or other. I've got to get to the bottom of it.'

'And how do you propose to do that? Private eye?'

'If necessary,' said Nikolai coolly.

Tom whistled. 'Oh, boy, has she got you boiling.'

'It won't be necessary,' Nikolai said with superb assurance. 'The Ivanovs still have contacts. I shall make a few calls; that's all.' Suddenly a lot less cool, he said, 'And then I'll find out every damned thing there is to know about Lisa Romaine.'

'And then what?' said Tom, ever practical. 'Even if she turns out to be the daughter of Fu Manchu, what do you think you can do about it? From Borneo? Or even from France for that matter?'

Nikolai had already taken a decision on that one.

'I'm not going back to France. I'm staying right here in London until this is sorted out.'

Tom gaped. 'But you hate London.'

'I hate being beaten even more,' Nikolai said with truth. 'No ragamuffin is going to move in on my aunt without a fight.'

'What you mean is, this girl isn't going to get the better of you,' Tom said shrewdly.

Nikolai smiled. It was not a pleasant smile. 'You are so right.'

Lisa had gone home, muttering. Tatiana was out in the garden but Lisa didn't want to talk to her. So she shut the

French windows firmly and turned her attention to her week's housekeeping.

To help her along she played the latest Ibiza compilation loudly. She had put a second load of washing into the machine and was bopping happily round the sitting room with the elderly vacuum cleaner that Tatiana had supplied when the phone rang.

Lisa switched off the vacuum cleaner and regarded the phone balefully.

'Nikolai Ivanov, I will tell your aunt on you.'

But it was not Nikolai. It was her mother. And she was fighting back tears.

'I'll come at once,' said Lisa, when she'd heard what Joanne Romaine had to say.

As soon as she'd been able to afford it, Lisa had moved her mother and sister out of their Bow tenement into a small semi-detached house in the suburbs. It was easy enough to visit after work, when the commuter trains were still running, but on a Sunday the trains were few and far between. Lisa called a minicab.

Joanne was waiting. She hugged Lisa convulsively.

'What's happened?' said Lisa, hugging her back.

She tried not to sound resigned. Kit had been anorexic in her early teens, and ever since her mother had been braced for it to happen again. Lisa sometimes wondered if Kit's problems were caused as much by Joanne's hyper-anxiety as anything else. But she was too loyal to say so.

Joanna's mouth was pinched. 'Kit hasn't had a meal with me this week.'

'Oh, dear,' said Lisa. She had lived at home until she was eighteen. She knew the signs that her sister's eating disorder was reviving. Maybe on this occasion her mother was not overreacting.

'I rang the college.' Kit was doing a course in computer studies. 'The student counsellor more or less called me an over-anxious mother.' She paused dramatically. 'And then she said that everything was all right now.'

'Now?' Lisa was bewildered.

Joanne's eyes were strained. 'Kit has been dating one of the older students. The counsellor said they keep an eye on him because they're worried about drugs. So they know the last two college discos he's come with another girl. So—'

'He's dumped her,' said Lisa.

She was already on her way up the stairs.

Kit was sitting on the floor, listening to Pan pipes and staring into space. Lisa hesitated in the doorway.

'Can I come in?'

Kit looked up vaguely. 'Oh, hi, Lisa,' she said. She showed neither surprise nor interest. 'Sure.'

Lisa pulled a pretty cushion off the bed and pushed it behind her back as she too slipped down onto the carpet and leaned back against the leg of the bed. She knew better than to ask how Kit was.

'You really like this stuff?' she said, jerking her head at the stereo she had given Kit for Christmas.

Kit smiled, but it was clearly an effort. Lisa was shocked by her appearance. She didn't say so. Instead she demanded, 'What on earth do you dance to? I mean, you can't boogie to something that sounds like a dentist's drill.'

Kit's eyes were agonised. 'I don't dance.'

'How do you get out of it? I thought student life was one long disco these days.'

'Only if you're pretty,' muttered Kit.

Lisa was silenced. She knew there was no point in telling Kit that her corn-gold hair and greeny grey eyes were charms that many girls would have killed for. When she was down like this Kit hated herself and was deeply suspicious of anyone who found anything good to say about her.

Lisa sought for some topic to deflect Kit from her self-punishing despair.

'Did I tell you I'm up for an award?' she said at last in desperation.

Kit knew nothing about Lisa's work, and could not have

cared less about the world of finance. But the sisters had always taken pleasure in each other's successes.

'Great. What is it?'

'Trader of the Year. It's presented at the annual Association dinner on Tuesday. It's going to be the pits, because I won't know until the end whether I've won or not.'

Kit became more alert. 'You'll win,' she said stoutly.

Lisa pulled a face. 'Maybe. I have to write a thank-you speech anyway, just in case.' She paused. 'You know, I could really do with some support.'

Kit was startled. 'Like what?'

'Well, do you think Mother and you might come?' Lisa suggested cunningly.

Kit could very often be persuaded to do things for her mother and sister that she would not do for herself. Lisa paused hopefully.

Kit looked away, not answering.

'I know it's boring. But it would mean a lot to me.' Even as she said it, Lisa realised that it was true.

Kit seemed to realise it too. 'Why?'

'Because my boss won't come; that's for sure.'

Lisa realised that she hadn't known until now how much she minded about that.

'He won't be able to resist giving me a public slap in the face.'

'Why would he do that?' said Kit, concerned.

'He's never liked me since—'

Since she'd had an affair with Terry Long.

'He worked for Terry too,' Lisa muttered.

Kit nodded with understanding. She knew more about Lisa's romantic disaster than anyone.

Lisa had been eighteen, riding on top of the world as she'd begun to realise she not only liked her job, she was good at it. The department had started sending her on courses. She'd seen the sort of career she had never imagined opening up before her. And then Terry Long had arrived.

Terry had been a man on the way up. As a boss he'd been inspiring, not just to Lisa but to Sam Voss and everyone else on the team as well. As a man he was an unscrupulous serial charmer. Lisa had had no defences against him at all.

'But Terry went to New York ages ago,' objected Kit.

'Three years. But Sam doesn't forgive. He thinks office affairs are unprofessional and I should never have let it happen.'

'Stupid man,' said Kit. 'You don't want him coming to your dinner anyway.'

Lisa gave a reluctant laugh. 'I'd rather he didn't advertise to the whole City how much he disapproves of me, though.'

'His loss. More important—' her voice came to life '—what are you going to wear?'

Lisa was taken aback. 'Hey, it's not the Oscars, you know.'

'It is for you. And you have to show everyone that you don't care.' Suddenly mischievous, she said, 'Crimson silk and diamonds.'

Pleased, Lisa grinned. 'Not my style,' she said firmly. 'Or the Association's, for that matter. The men will all wear dinner jackets and the women are supposed to look as much like men as they can. So I'll find something dark and respectable.'

'No diamonds?' asked Kit, disappointed.

'Maybe one day. Can't afford them yet.'

Kit's face froze. 'You spend too much on us, don't you? Especially me. All those therapies and consultants.'

'Of course not,' said Lisa, furious with herself.

'Don't lie,' said Kit. 'That last clinic I went to—you said it was a charity. But everyone else who was there was a rich kid.'

'Rich kids get sick too,' said Lisa defensively.

'Yes, and their daddies pay the bill for their treatment. And in my case you were doing it. Weren't you?'

Lisa made a great business of plumping up the cushion behind her. 'Health is important.'

But Kit shook her head and fell silent. In the end Lisa gave up and went downstairs.

'I blew it,' she said to her mother glumly. She told her the salient facts.

'She may come. It takes her time to talk herself into these things,' said Joanne, trying to look on the bright side, as always. She patted Lisa's arm. 'Get us both a ticket, anyway. I'll talk to her.'

The kettle began to boil. Joanne put teabags into the pot and poured the boiling stream of water onto them.

'Everything seemed to be going so well,' she said, concentrating. 'But of course if there was a man...'

Lisa made an exasperated noise. Joanne stirred the tea.

'Yes, I know you think men are a waste of time,' Joanna said with a touch of defiance. 'But we're not all like you, you know. Kit's very vulnerable.'

Lisa snorted again. 'Everyone's vulnerable if they let themselves be mucked around.'

'It's not always a question of *letting*,' said her mother drily.

Lisa was briefly conscience-stricken. Their father had left Joanne soon after Kit was born. Lisa didn't remember him at all. What she could remember was that Joanne had never looked at another man since, all through the struggle with poverty that had been their childhood.

'I'm sorry,' she said, contrite. 'It's just—I don't see how anyone can take men seriously. My boss is so jealous of me it's transparent, Alec has behaved like a spoiled child, and today I met a man who looks like he walked out of a dream. And he turns out to be the worst of the lot.' She gave an angry laugh.

Joanne looked at her thoughtfully. 'Who is this dreamboat?'

Lisa shrugged impatiently. 'Just some interfering relation of my new landlady.'

'Oh.' Joanne digested this in silence.

She poured tea and took the two mugs into the sitting room. Outside the rain was pelting down, but Joanne stood at the window and watched the soaked garden with pleasure. Lisa took the tea from her, smiling.

They had lived in a succession of rooms and flats in the poorest parts of London. Until Lisa had bought this house Joanne had never owned her own home, still less a garden. Now, every time she passed the window and saw trees, she stopped to marvel at it.

Lisa felt her eyes moisten and blinked. She was not sentimental, she told herself fiercely. She was *not*.

Joanne tore herself away from her garden and sat down.

'So how did you meet the interfering relation?' she asked.

'What?' Lisa had been briefly back in her slum childhood. She gave herself a little shake and returned to the present. 'Oh, Boris. He came pounding on the door this morning, when I was still in bed.'

Joanne bit back a smile. She knew Lisa's weekend rising habits. 'Then I'm surprised you still think he's a dreamboat.'

'It's not exactly a matter of opinion,' said Lisa wryly. 'He fulfils the job description. Tall, dark and handsome. Even quite nice when he puts his mind to it.'

'And you hate him,' said Joanne, interpreting Lisa's tone with the ease of long practice. 'Just because he got you out of bed?'

Lisa gave her sudden grin. 'It didn't help,' she admitted.

'Poor man,' said Joanne with feeling.

'Don't waste your pity. Nikolai Ivanov doesn't need it.'

'I thought his name was Boris,' said Joanne, bewildered.

'That's what I called him. He didn't like it.' Lisa dwelled on the memory with evident satisfaction.

'It sounds as if you had quite a conversation.'

'Oh, he took me out to lunch.'

'He took—' Joanne stared. 'How long have you known this man?'

'I told you. We met this morning when he got me out of bed.'

'And you still had lunch with him?' Joanne was impressed. She knew Lisa's tactics with men. Since the Terry Long episode she kept them at arm's length for several months before she agreed to have so much as cup of coffee with them. 'He must be a world-class dreamboat.'

'He's a world-class pig,' snapped Lisa, her face darkening.

'And what does he think of you?' murmured Joanne, entertained.

Lisa showed her teeth. 'I'm an out and out con artist and he doesn't like my table manners.'

'*What?*' said Joanne, losing her amusement.

'Not that much of a dreamboat, huh?' said Lisa.

'He must be out of his mind.'

'No,' said Lisa fair-mindedly, 'I provoked him. He thought he could charm me and I—showed him he was wrong.'

Joanne nodded slowly. 'I can see that you would.' She gave Lisa a sudden, brilliant smile. 'No man is ever going to charm you into losing your judgement, is he, pet?'

'No,' said Lisa.

She didn't say, Not again. She did not need to.

She was reminded of the conversation next morning. Her mother, she thought, should see this.

'You've nearly missed the chance to go on television,' Rob told her as she came out of the mid-morning meeting. He was grinning. 'Gary's ready to stand in for you, though.' He chuckled. 'He's gone out to get highlights in his hair.'

Lisa paused in the act of sitting down at her computer screen. 'You're joking.'

'No. The TV crew will be here at twelve. Bet he tops up the tan as well.' He raised his voice so the rest of the team could hear him. 'Five to one Gary comes back browner than he went.'

There was a derisive chorus. The odds shortened and notes changed hands.

'He'll be ready to kill when he finds you're back after all,' said Rob with satisfaction.

He was right.

'Of course, you're the Head of Bond Trading,' Gary said huffily. The television lights glinted on his newly lacquered hair. 'You should do it.'

Lisa's eyes danced. 'But you've got yourself up so prettily,' she said.

'What do you mean?'

'Just that you're a natural for the guru-to-camera bit,' she told him soothingly. 'You'll do it much better than I would.'

This was greeted with raucous laughter. Gary flushed.

'Just because you don't take care of yourself,' he said spitefully. 'It's not my fault you look a mess.'

Lisa stopped smiling. 'Thank you for your style analysis.'

She sat down and turned her back on him. Gary shrugged, and went to talk to the television camera. Lisa ignored him, concentrating on the screen.

Rob peered over the top of his own screen. 'Gary's a prat,' he offered eventually.

Lisa nodded, not answering.

Rob tried again. 'Are you taking anyone to the Association dinner tomorrow?'

'My mother and sister,' Lisa said airily.

Rob looked dissatisfied. 'If you need a man...' he began.

His attempt at delicacy made Lisa wince. 'I do not,' she yelled, 'need a man.'

From across the room, the US Dollar exchange dealers raised a cheer.

One of them called out, 'Get your hands off her, Rob, you pathetic lecher. Don't you know she's one of the boys?'

In Sam Voss's office, his visitor looked up, arrested.

Lisa didn't know she was being watched. Her anger dissolved in laughter at their teasing.

'Bunch of sexist pigs,' she said peacefully.

Rob drew a relieved breath. 'What happens at the dinner?'

'Eat a lot, try not to drink too much in case I win. Listen to a lot of boring speeches. And, if I win, they hand over the statuary and I get my turn in the boring speech stakes. Oh, and I get to be kissed by God.'

Rob laughed. 'Or God's stand-in.'

The guest of honour at the Association's dinner was a politician whose financial affairs were currently under investigation by the newspapers. The dealing room, highly entertained, was running a book on his chances of surviving long enough to present the awards.

'They'll have trouble getting anyone else at this short notice,' said Lisa.

'Oh, no problem. They'll call Rent-a-Nob,' said Rob.

'Oh, wow,' said Lisa cynically. 'The honour of it. I can hardly bear it.'

The screens began to flicker again. All round the room people leaned forward, scanning the incoming message. Under cover of the preoccupation, Lisa looked over the top of the bank of screens in front of her.

'Thanks, Rob,' she said quietly.

Nikolai had used Lisa's business card to good effect. The result was that he had decided further investigations would take longer than he had planned on. Certainly too long to stay in a hotel, however luxurious. Nikolai hated hotels.

So he had called some friends. By Monday morning he'd had the offer of a number of flats. By Monday lunchtime he had moved into one, courtesy of a geology professor whose mother had made her summer move to Scotland. It was old-fashioned, and further away from the Royal Geographical Society Library than he wanted, but it had the bonus of being just round the corner from Tatiana.

By Monday afternoon, responses to his other calls had started to come in.

'Count Ivanov? Roger Maurice here. I edit *Financial Monthly*. I've been asked to give you a call.'

'Really?' said Nikolai without enthusiasm. He didn't like journalists on principle.

'I gather we might be able to help each other,' said Roger Maurice. 'You want to know about Lisa Romaine. Well, I've just done a piece on top tarts in the City. What do you want to know?'

Nikolai was taken aback. 'She's *that* well known?'

'And successful.'

'Good heavens.'

'Not an entirely unsullied career path, I gather,' said Roger Maurice delicately. 'Good results. But sometimes a bit of a question mark over how she gets her promotion. I could give you some people to talk to. And in return…'

He explained.

Nikolai's unseen smile was triumphant. Oh, he was going to show Lisa Romaine what it was like to cross a man who was not misled by big green eyes or afraid of political incorrectness. Some men were still masters of themselves. As she was going to learn to her cost.

Maurice read out some phone numbers. 'And tomorrow night? Can we count on your help?'

'I regard it as a debt of honour,' Nikolai said.

He meant it.

Kit rang to say she wouldn't be able to get to the presentation dinner at five o'clock. Lisa argued, but her sister was adamant. In the end Kit hung up on her. Lisa called her mother.

'I'm sorry, love,' said Joanne, who clearly already knew Kit's decision. 'I told you she's been in a funny mood. I don't think I'd better come either. I don't want to leave her alone.'

Lisa didn't say anything. Suddenly her pleasure in the evening dimmed.

'What about leaving *me* alone?' she muttered. But not so her mother could hear.

But Joanne picked up something. 'Do you mind? Will it ruin your evening?'

Lisa suppressed a sigh. 'No.'

Joanne didn't hear the disappointment. She said hearteningly, 'Have a wonderful time, then. And drink some champagne for me.'

'I will.'

So Lisa went along with Rob after all. She hid her loneliness under outrageous earrings that brushed her shoulders and a velvet jacket borrowed from Sam's secretary.

'Just don't take it off,' said Angela, brushing lint off the lapels in the ladies' cloakroom. 'Your gear is great for dancing, but it will give the old boys a heart attack if they see all that flesh.'

Lisa turned this way and that in front of the mirror.

'Is Sam coming?' she asked casually.

Angela put the brush back on the vanity unit. She didn't look at Lisa.

'He bought a ticket.'

'That's not what I asked.'

'I think there's some sort of crisis at home,' said poor Angela, torn between loyalty to her boss and sympathy for Lisa.

Lisa tossed her blonde head. 'You don't have to dress it up for me,' she said in a light, hard tone. 'I knew he wouldn't come. No boss. No family. Oh, well, *Financial Monthly* thinks I'm the greatest. What else can I want?'

She sashayed into the panelled hall, hung with portraits of aldermen and city company flags, like a woman bent on challenging all comers. Rob eyed her uneasily. He didn't know this glittering, dangerous mood but he had a bad feeling about it.

He took a couple of glasses from a waiter's tray and

handed her one, looking round. The tall room was still half empty.

'Quiet this year.'

Lisa's green eyes narrowed like a cat's seeking prey. She gave the slow grin that sent shivers up the spine of bosses and opponents alike. 'Soon change that.'

Rob took a gulp of his drink. 'What do you mean?' he said, alarmed.

But she laughed and didn't answer.

'Don't do anything stupid,' he begged.

She raised her chin, and the light shone on her newly washed blonde cap of hair. Rob hardly noticed.

'I mean it,' he said urgently. 'Don't think Sam won't find out, just because he isn't here. All his cronies are. If you start dancing on tables they'll all be on their mobiles.'

Lisa gave a private grin. Rob felt the hairs on the back of his neck rise.

Lisa—' he began warningly.

'OK. OK,' she said impatiently. 'No dancing on tables. At least,' she added naughtily, 'not here. Fancy going out later?'

Rob nodded, relieved. And then other people began to arrive and he and Lisa were separated by the crowd.

They didn't get together again until they sat down for dinner. She seemed to have calmed down, he saw with relief. But then she picked up the programme. He felt her go utterly still.

'What is it?'

Lisa looked up slowly. Her eyes were blank. Then it seemed to poor Rob that even as he looked at her she began to quiver, very, very gently, like grass in the wind before an earthquake.

'Oh, dear,' he said.

He looked round for something to account for this terrible rage.

The caterers had done their best to keep up with the cancellations at the Napier Kraus table. They had removed two covers, but Sam's no-show had thrown them. As a result Lisa was sitting next to an empty chair. Worse, the place-card said 'Kit Romaine'.

Rob palmed it swiftly. But Lisa's shivering fury seemed to stem from something else entirely.

'The guest of honour,' she said between her teeth.

'What?'

She could hardly get it out. 'Oh, boy, have Rent-a-Nob come up with a lulu.'

Rob looked at the proceedings card in the middle of the table.

'"Count Nikolai Ivanov",' he read. He looked up. 'Who's he?'

'Count!' Lisa was so angry she could barely speak.

Rob was none the wiser. One of their fellow diners leaned forward.

'Explorer chap. Bit of a coup getting him. Especially at short notice.'

Lisa snorted.

'No, really. He doesn't usually do after-dinner speaking.'

'All explorers do after-dinner speaking,' said Lisa flatly. She had sat through a fair number of after-dinner speeches since she joined Napier Kraus. 'They're as bad as politicians. It's all in support of the great cause of fundraising.'

Their companion chuckled. 'Shouldn't think an Ivanov needs to raise funds. Plenty of Swiss bank accounts there.'

For some reason the news seemed to make Lisa even more mad, Rob saw. She barely spoke during the course of the meal. Only when the guest speaker rose to his feet did she seem to come out of her black absorption. In fact she sat bolt upright, and turned a laser glare on him.

It must have felt like a flame-thrower, thought Rob with sympathy. Certainly Nikolai Ivanov seemed to be looking towards their table more often than he looked anywhere else. And when he announced that Lisa was the Trader of the Year and picked up her prize to present it—

Lisa got up and slipped off her jacket. Under the jacket

she was wearing a low-backed, cropped silver top. In the staid atmosphere it made her look shockingly young. She tilted her gleaming head at Nikolai in silent challenge.

Nikolai stayed impassive. But he knew, as she did, that neither of them saw anyone else in the room. And as she turned to make her way round an intervening table he saw that the low back revealed a tattooed butterfly on the point of flight nestling below her left shoulderblade

Suddenly the duel between them was charged with something a lot more primitive. His pulse gave one great thud, like the impact of an axe on an anvil. And then he felt his blood begin to beat hot and hard. As Lisa prowled up the steps of the podium, like a cat on the hunt, she did not know it but she faced lust incarnate.

Nikolai remained impassive, though it was an effort. She was not going to see how strongly he needed to get his hands on her. Or not yet. Later, maybe.

He picked up the small statuette and gave her his blandest smile. Lisa's eyes turned black with fury. 'Congratulations,' Nikolai said deliberately.

To Lisa's outrage he reached out and took her unresponsive hand. As the room applauded, he shook it heartily.

'I'm told this is very well deserved.'

'Thank you.' She sounded as if it would choke her.

Nikolai's eyes gleamed. He gave her the statuette. Then, to Lisa's blank astonishment, he put an arm round her and pulled her beside him to face the room.

A dart of electricity shot through her, so strong she gasped. She flinched away from him. But the dinner-jacketed arm was stronger than she'd expected. She was clamped ruthlessly to his side.

Lisa turned her head and glared. 'Take your hands off me.' She did not bother to lower her voice.

The continuing applause drowned her words. So only Nikolai heard. He began to enjoy himself. Although the thunder in his blood had not diminished with his arm round her, he realised that Lisa was too angry to recognise the condition he was in. Relaxing, he looked down at her.

'Smile for the cameras,' he said kindly.

Lisa could have screamed. But she held still while the photographer took a number of pictures. Then she made an acceptance speech so brief that the applause was genuinely appreciative. She turned her back and walked away from Nikolai without a second look.

Nikolai watched the butterfly on her shoulderblade. He made himself a silent promise. He was going to kiss that provocative tattoo. Preferably tonight.

Lisa didn't see any of the faces as she walked away from the podium. Her whole body tingled as if she had walked into an electric fence. She felt stunned.

She would have felt better if she had seen the look in Nikolai's eyes as he watched her. Rob, who did, was startled. He recognised naked hunger when he saw it.

So he was not surprised when, as the formal part of the evening finished and people began to circulate between tables, Nikolai made his way towards them. Rob touched Lisa on the arm.

She looked up. Nikolai was not looking at her as he made his way through the crowd. He was receiving compliments, answering questions, even—once—autographing a menu. But never, for a moment, did he halt his steady advance in her direction.

Lisa went very still.

'Stick with me, Rob,' she said in an urgent under-voice.

It was so unlike the Lisa he knew that Rob was startled. And then Nikolai was upon them.

'Miss Romaine. How nice to see you again.'

It must have taken generations of aristocratic breeding to produce that particular tone, Lisa thought, raging. The courtesy was so false he didn't try to disguise it.

It was like a game, and he was master of it. Well, she never turned down a dare. Her chin lifted.

'You're luckier than I am, then,' she said, with calculated rudeness. 'I hoped I'd seen the last of you.'

Rob winced. Nikolai smiled and ignored him.

'Really? Hardly likely in the circumstances.' And the look he gave her was almost caressing.

What circumstances? thought Rob. He scented potential embarrassment. It alarmed him. Exactly as Nikolai had intended it to.

Rob began to back away, murmuring excuses. Lisa didn't notice. All her attention was on the enemy.

'You mean you've got a reputation for hounding women?' she challenged him, her jaw jutting.

'I have a reputation for finishing what I start,' he corrected gently.

'You have not,' said Lisa between her teeth, 'started anything with me.'

He was unmoved. 'I think we both know that's not true.'

He pulled out Kit's unused chair and swung the little gilt thing round as if it was no heavier than an umbrella. He sat astride it, his hands along the back, his chin on his hands. And looked at her.

Lisa could feel the interested eyes. Normally she didn't care—or even notice—when people stared at her. But in this gathering, under this man's blatant scrutiny, she felt uncomfortable. More than uncomfortable. And furious.

'Nonsense,' she said curtly.

His eyes crinkled up at the corners when he laughed.

'Then why did you take this off?'

'What?'

In silent answer he lifted the jacket half off the back of her chair with one long finger.

'What?'

He let his eyes rest on her shadowed cleavage.

'Were you reminding me that we still haven't settled the matter of your bra size?' he said, amused.

His eyes lifted. Lisa read challenge, and laughter, and—

To her horror, she felt her face heat at the other things she saw in his face.

'Don't,' she said involuntarily.

And was instantly furious with herself. How dared he do this to her? Oh, how dared he?

'What are you doing after this?' he murmured.

Lisa was too shaken by her own feelings to think of anything subtle. 'None of your business,' she snapped.

He smiled as if she had told him what he wanted to know. 'I *thought* you weren't the type to go home to bed,' he said complacently. 'Which club?'

Lisa took hold of herself. She didn't fluster easily, she reminded herself. No one sent her into blushing retreat. *No one.*

So she leaned back on her gilt chair and looked him up and down with slow insolence.

'Oh, you wouldn't get into any of the clubs my friends and I go to,' she drawled.

He raised his eyebrows. His eyes were brown and soft as velvet and faintly preoccupied. As if he was imagining them alone, kissing, more than kissing... The way he looked at her, he could have been running his hand over her naked skin. He could have been...

'Stop it,' said Lisa under her breath.

Nikolai laughed. 'Will you tell the club to throw me out?' he teased softly. The tone was seduction all on its own.

Lisa swallowed and pulled herself together.

'No need,' she said hardily. 'You're too old.'

His eyes narrowed sharply, the seductive preoccupation banished. For a moment she thought she had scored a hit. But then he shook his head in reproach.

'That isn't kind.'

'The truth often isn't.'

'I don't believe they'd bar me on the grounds of senility.'

Neither did Lisa, to tell the truth. She said hurriedly, 'Anyway, you're dressed all wrong.'

He was laughing openly now. 'How much do I need to take off to dress acceptably, then?'

Lisa blinked. He tipped his chair forward until his mouth was almost brushing her ear.

'I can take my clothes off, too, you know,' he murmured huskily.

Lisa jumped out of her chair as if he had branded her, and hauled her jacket round her shoulders. Nikolai laughed.

Lisa was horrified. She felt as if she was in freefall: nothing stable, everything that she'd thought certain whirling round her head, lost and humiliated and out of control. She had not felt like that since she was eighteen.

Not since the night that Terry, too, had laughed at her.

She couldn't help herself. She sent Nikolai one dismayed look. And bolted.

CHAPTER FOUR

Left behind, Nikolai stood up. The laughter died out of his face, leaving it set and determined. He watched her go, his eyes hard. But Lisa did not see that.

Rob did, however. He already had a conscience about abandoning Lisa. So he moved to intercept the unpredictable guest of honour.

'I wouldn't.' His tone was quite friendly but the determination was unmistakable.

Slowly Nikolai withdrew his gaze from Lisa's retreating figure. He looked, thought Rob, as if he had forgotten that there was anyone but Lisa and himself in the room. Rob positioned himself squarely in front of him.

'Excuse me?' said Nikolai blankly.

'Leave the girl alone.'

Nikolai stiffened.

'I beg your pardon?'

Rob repeated it.

Nikolai's eyes narrowed. 'And you are?'

For some obscure reason, under those hard eyes Rob felt he had to justify himself. 'Just a friend,' he said hastily. 'But Lisa's in a funny mood tonight. She was already upset because—well, someone she wanted to be here cried off at the last moment. I really wouldn't push it if I were you.'

There was a glacial pause.

'Wouldn't you?' Nikolai said sardonically.

Rob had a sudden, hair-raising picture of what Lisa in her present mood would do if Nikolai Ivanov kept after her tonight.

'There's a support group for men who have tried to hit

on Lisa Romaine,' Rob told him, stampeded into honesty
by simple panic. 'And that's on her good days. Leave it.'

'Thank you for your advice,' said Nikolai without expression.

He shouldered his way past Rob without another word.

Nikolai was in a cold rage. What game was she playing?
She knew as well as he did that the attraction between them
made the air crackle. And she was a modern girl, tough and
uncompromising. So why the *hell* did she keep walking
away from it?

Well, he wasn't going to walk away from it. And neither
was Lisa Romaine. He would not let her.

Lisa circulated frantically. She received dozens of congrat-
ulatory kisses on the cheek. In her wake, the photographer
clicked busily. She talked all the time in a high, rapid voice,
as if by talking she could ward off the inevitable. Her eyes
were restless, but she never once looked behind her. And
she never once mentioned Nikolai Ivanov either.

Eventually she caught up with Rob again.

'Ready to party?'

He looked at her feverish expression. 'Wouldn't you
rather go home?'

'Home? Me? Nonsense. I'm on a roll. No one,' she said
with emphasis, 'is going to stop me having fun tonight.'

Rob did not misinterpret. 'Don't worry. He left ages ago.'

'He? Who?'

'The Count you hate.'

Lisa tossed her head. 'I don't hate Nikolai Ivanov. I don't
care a snap of my fingers for him.'

She suited the action to her words, clicking her fingers
under his nose. Rob jumped back nervously.

'Well, he left.'

'I don't care what he does,' Lisa said untruthfully. Her
glitter seemed to dim a little. 'I'm going to have a ball. Just
let me loosen up a little and we can get going.'

She emerged from the cloakroom five minutes later with

her hair greased into rainbow spikes. She had shed her skirt for designer jeans but she had put her jacket back on over the silver cut-away top. Rob took note of the necklace like a silver halter and new earrings made from multi-coloured paper clips. She looked sharp and ready for anything. He went towards her.

'They've just called your name. They seem to have got you a cab.'

Lisa pulled a surprised face. 'Prizewinner's perks, I suppose. Great. Let's hit the night.' She saw an Australian colleague from another bank. 'Want to come on to a club, Andy?' she called.

In the end six of them piled into the limousine. They went to Deep South, a club in central London. It was new and trendy and they had all been there on its opening night. The bouncer on the door nodded them in without hassle.

Lisa slid through a narrow doorway into the ladies' cloakroom. With the speed of familiarity she transferred money, scent and mascara from her handbag into a tiny pouch that she secured round her waist. Then she stuffed everything, including bag, jacket and the award statuette, into her briefcase and checked it in return for a kiss-shaped tag. She thrust the garish token into her pouch and zipped it tight. Then, hips and shoulders already moving to the beat, she made for the music.

Eighty strenuous minutes later she felt wonderful. She had danced with Rob, with the others, on her own and with complete strangers. Hurt, annoyance and even her worry about Kit evaporated. Only Nikolai Ivanov hovered at the edge of her consciousness, and she refused to think about him until tomorrow.

She danced like a flickering flame. People noticed, admiring or hungry. She deflected an inexpert pass from a youth in baggy shorts, then saw off another, more determined foray. Both of them made her laugh. She could never stay mad when she was dancing.

'Drink?' yelled Andy, dancing over to her.

Lisa nodded, eyes bright. But she didn't follow him from the dance floor. Andy grinned and step-danced round a noisy group in the direction of the bar.

Alone on the floor, Lisa flung back her head and punched her arms exuberantly in the air. Her face was absorbed. Her limbs pumped to the beat as if they were oiled. In the cavernous lighting, her skin glowed.

To the tall man on the gallery, she looked possessed by the music. As he watched she laughed aloud with sheer physical pleasure. Its effect on him was stark and immediate.

I want her to look like that when I make love to her, Nikolai thought.

The music throbbed. The glittering light balls in the roof wheeled, stippling the dancers with a shower of diamond rain. Lisa felt a touch in the small of her back. Another pass, she thought tolerantly. One prudent hand went to protect the pouch at her waist as she turned, still dancing. The new arrival, his face masked by the pulsing shadows, saw it and shook his head at her suspicions. He gave her an opened bottle of water.

'Thanks,' mouthed Lisa.

The plastic bottle was ice cold. She drank, then held it gratefully against her neck. The man danced closer.

She tipped her head back to look at him in the half-dark. He was expertly dressed for the club's tropical atmosphere, Lisa saw, in loose cotton trousers and some sort of sleeveless khaki waistcoat. It was open and she saw a powerfully ribbed chest underneath, roughened by a dusting of dark hair. And he moved as if he'd been born dancing.

Lisa didn't often dance with men who were as good as she was. After a moment's shock, she laughed aloud with delight. She began to move with him, deliberately rotating her shoulders to mimic his movements. When he touched and turned her, she felt a heady sense of energy, as if together they made a super-charged machine.

And he was tireless. Normally Lisa could dance anyone

off the floor. But this time it was she who flagged. He saw it. At once he put a masterful arm round her waist and walked her off the floor in front of him. His strength made Lisa's pulses beat harder than the music.

Halfway up the spiral staircase she looked over her shoulder.

'All right, you've proved your point,' she said, trying to sound normal.

Nikolai took her empty water bottle away from her.

'They let me in after all, you see,' he agreed, smiling down into her hot eyes.

Lisa looked at the tanned, muscular arms, the deep chest. Her heart did an uncomfortable back-flip. *Damn!*

'Probably scared not to,' she whipped back. She might be shaken but she recovered fast. 'You look a complete thug.'

Nikolai gave a bark of laughter. 'But not an *old* thug?' he challenged.

Lisa was prevented from answering by a group of new arrivals descending the staircase. Nikolai's arm crushed her to him as they pressed past. The unimpassioned embrace left her shockingly short of breath.

'What are you doing here?' she said, when she could speak again. Her voice rasped in her throat. To her annoyance she had to cough to clear it. 'Slumming, Count Ivanov?'

'Following you,' he said, with complete sang-froid.

'Wh—what?'

He let her go and looked down into her shocked green eyes with a quizzical expression.

'I've got designs on your tattoo,' he murmured in a thrilling under-voice.

Lisa gulped.

'Why else would I be in a place like this?'

Another couple squeezed past them, pressing them together with shocking intimacy. Lisa jerked in shock.

'You know, I hate to say this, but don't you think we

should move?' Nikolai murmured. 'It's a bit antisocial to block the stairway like this.'

'What?' Lisa was fighting to return her breathing to normal.

'Move,' he said softly, his lips a feather's distance from her ear.

She gave a long, slow shudder. 'Oh. Yes.'

In disarray she ran up the rest of the ironwork stairs. Her head whirled.

How could he have followed her? How? He had left the reception long before she did. And none of the others could have told him they were coming to Deep South. They hadn't decided until they were already in the limousine.

Nikolai said, 'Are you ready to go?'

Lisa stiffened. 'And what does that mean?'

He smiled down at her, his eyes swooningly near. 'I'm taking you home. As you very well know.'

Her expression was stubborn. 'I go home with the man who brought me. You didn't.'

'True,' he agreed, not noticeably cast down. 'Three of the guys you came with have gone already. The others know I'm taking you home.'

Lisa stiffened. 'I'm not a parcel you can pass round between you. I go home alone.'

He shook his head. 'No way.'

'I—beg—your—pardon?' said Lisa dangerously.

Nikolai was unmoved. 'Get your coat.'

He touched her arm. Lisa shook him off. But the beat was getting heavier and her watch told her it was nearly three. She had to admit it was time to go. She slid away from him and went to the cloakroom.

He was waiting for her when she emerged. Without waiting for her permission, he took possession of her briefcase and shouldered his way out.

It had stopped raining but there were wide puddles on the pavement. Streetlights, traffic lights, and neon shop signs glittered up at them in shards of reflection. The street was nearly deserted. A group of revellers ran along the opposite pavement, oblivious to anything but their own noise. Two policemen passed, their measured tread loud in the pre-dawn lull.

Standing outside the club with Nikolai Ivanov, Lisa felt strangely insulated from the rest of the world. It was as if being together in the chill end of the night somehow made them intimate. Like survivors, she thought.

In a darkened doorway a pair of lovers clung. Their limbs were indistinguishable one from the other in the shadowy embrace. Lisa was suddenly hot and cold at the same time. She shivered and looked away.

Nikolai didn't notice. He raised a hand.

'Taxis don't just cruise at this time of night,' Lisa informed him, with satisfaction. 'Not here. You have to—'

A grey limousine came a silent halt at the kerb.

'—phone for a minicab,' she finished lamely.

Nikolai smiled down at her and opened the car door. Lisa didn't like it. But, as she'd said, taxis were hard to come by in the small hours. She got in.

'I suppose you called for one while I was in the cloakroom,' she muttered, annoyed.

'Stanley Crescent,' Nikolai told the driver. He got in beside her and slid a lazy arm along the back of the seat behind her. 'On the contrary. The car has been on stand-by ever since you got to the club tonight.'

Lisa sniffed. 'More of your famous planning, I suppose.' She was scornful.

'Quite.'

And then she did a double take. 'Ever since *I* got to the club?'

'Alfredo brought you,' Nikolai said blandly. 'How do you think I knew which club to come to?'

She swung round, outraged. 'You *spied* on me?'

'Just good planning.'

'From where I'm sitting,' said Lisa, with heat, 'it feels like spying.'

He leaned back, very much at his ease. 'And why should that worry you?' He paused. 'If you've got nothing to hide.'

Lisa narrowed her eyes at him. 'Be very careful,' she told him softly. 'I don't bully easily.'

'And you fight dirty,' he agreed, amused. 'I remember you warned me.' His eyes flicked up and down her body, registering the glimpse of pale flesh under her jacket. 'And I believe it. Just the way you dress gives you an unfair advantage.'

Lisa wanted to hit him so much she had to shut her eyes to stop him seeing it. She pulled the jacket tight round her.

'I dress to stay cool,' she informed him sharply. 'It's a sweaty business, dancing.'

'When you dance like you do, certainly.' He smiled. 'You put your whole heart and soul into it, don't you? I like a woman who throws herself into things.'

Oh, he was so *sure* of himself. Count Nikolai Ivanov, with his City contacts and his limousines on call! He thought he could loll there and insult her with clever innuendo and she couldn't do a thing to stop him.

She had no powerful friends, no limitless funds, no social position. She had nothing to fight him with. Nothing but her wits and her determination. Lisa saw the lounging figure through a red mist of rage.

'I will make you sorry,' she said between clenched teeth.

'For giving you a ride home when you would never have found a cab? Except maybe dressed like that, you would.' And he laughed. He *laughed*.

Lisa launched herself at him then. She was way beyond clear thought. She just knew she couldn't bear his mockery one moment longer.

Nikolai blinked. She didn't see him move. But he caught her flying hands easily. And held her still.

'Careful. You'll distract Alfredo.'

He held her in a strong grip. Lisa hauled against the restraint. Her eyes blazed.

'Let me go!' Lisa was beside herself. 'How dare you talk to me like that? Let me go at once.'

'Quiet!'

It was rapped out. The unconscious authority of it brought Lisa up short. She stopped fighting. Her eyes widened. She looked dazed.

Nikolai was surprised by the blank shock in her eyes. He didn't like it. Unexpectedly, he felt an unwelcome twinge of compunction. He dropped her hands.

Lisa rubbed her wrists automatically

'I'm sorry.' He was curt.

Lisa didn't answer. She retreated to the far end of the seat and turned her shoulder, staring out into the sodium-lit rainy night. She felt shaken to the core. She hadn't felt so frail, so vulnerable, since the night Terry had told her he was leaving.

I'll never forgive him, she thought. She leaned her hot forehead against the window and prayed to be home.

Nikolai looked at her with concern. Lisa punching her weight he could handle. Lisa reduced to devastated silence unnerved him.

'Are you all right?'

Lisa carried on staring out into the rain. The car glided silently along a tree-lined boulevard. In the dark, a distant park looked like a magic forest.

She remembered the suffocatingly narrow streets of her childhood, where there had been no trees at all. The man with her would have no idea at all of what that had been like. He would never have imagined sitting at a table, counting up the bills and the money, trying to balance the unbalanceable, knowing that if you bought Kit a pair of shoes the whole family would have to live on bread and milk for the rest of the week.

She said, almost inaudibly, 'I've come too far to let you turn me upside down.'

'What?'

Lisa shook her head. 'You wouldn't understand.'

'Try me,' said Nikolai, to his own surprise.

But still she didn't look at him. Or answer.

After a moment he said, 'I've rented an apartment. Let me give you coffee.'

She did look at him then. A bitterly ironic look.

'Just coffee,' he said, smiling.

'It's late. I have to be at work at seven.'

'Are you tired?'

Her shoulders lifted in a weary shrug.

'Of course I'm tired.'

'When you were dancing you looked as if nothing could tire you, ever.'

Lisa just looked at him.

'I've never seen anyone dance like you,' Nikolai said, to his own astonishment. This time he meant it and it wasn't an insult. 'You dance like a flame.'

But after what he had said earlier Lisa was not impressed. 'I still get tired like everyone else.'

The limousine cruised through a brief, brilliant oasis of lighted shops. Lisa leaned forward, not sure where she was. Then they turned right, leaving the lights for the shadows of pale Palladian terraces. Nikolai gave crisp directions. Alfredo took them round the railings of a garden square. The trees and bushes stirred in the night breeze.

'You have to be very rich to live with trees,' Lisa said, half to herself.

Nikolai was not sure he'd heard her. 'What was that?'

She didn't answer. At a word from Nikolai, Alfredo brought the limousine to a halt outside Tatiana's house. It was in darkness.

Lisa scrambled out onto the pavement. She reached back for her briefcase. And found that Nikolai was already out of the car, carrying it.

'If you won't come to me, then I'll take a coffee from you.'

It was an order. It sounded as if he was used to giving orders, Lisa thought. She did not waver.

'I need my sleep.'

He looked down at her. The faint breeze lifted her hair like a caress. His caress. He didn't move but Lisa felt as if he was touching her, just by the way he looked at her.

'And do you think you'll sleep if you go in alone now?' Nikolai said softly.

'Of course I—'

Without any warning, he dropped her briefcase and hauled her against him. Under her jacket, his hands were hot on the bared skin of her waist.

For a moment Lisa froze into immobility. Then she gave a muffled scream of fury and came alive. She writhed strenuously against his hold, pushing him away.

Nikolai drew a sharp breath. Briefly, the hard arms relaxed. For a moment she thought he was going to let her go. She stopped fighting...

He kissed her. Unexpected as a summer storm—and as fierce. His tongue probed and his hands were hard. And he was not teasing.

Lisa had been kissed more times than she could remember. Sometimes when she hadn't been expecting it. Even, once or twice, when she'd been angry. But never, *never* like this.

She could feel the determination in him. She pushed against him but her hands felt weak as water. Under the cotton waistcoat his chest was warm, in spite of being naked to the night air. The soft hairs were silky—another surprise—and shockingly pleasurable. The sensation made her shiver.

He felt it. Lisa heard him give a low growl of triumph. The strong hands tightened round her waist and then moved upwards, as if he were feeling for something. She felt his palm on her shoulderblade, possessive.

He moved her body so easily. It was as if she had no will or muscles of her own. As if he knew she had no ability to resist. Her head fell back, in spite of herself.

'Take me inside,' he murmured against her throat.

For a hectic moment she didn't know whether he meant her home or her body. Or both. And, crazily, did not care. She almost agreed to let him in and go wherever it took her...

But then she opened her eyes. Behind his head she saw the elegant sweep of the terrace, the chauffeur-driven car. A cold thought struck: this is a rich man playing a game. A clever game, but a game none the less. She had been here before and it hurt.

Nikolai felt her turn to a block of wood in his arms. He raised his head.

'What is it?'

Lisa didn't say anything. She didn't fight against his constraining hold. She simply stood there, locked in his arms, looking at him in the yellow streetlight.

He let her go. She didn't step away from him, but she was unresponsive to her fingertips.

'You change your mind fast,' Nikolai said. Anger licked through the smooth tones.

Lisa picked up her briefcase.

'No, I don't. I've always said I didn't want to have anything to do with you.' To her own astonishment she sounded quite cool about it. Even self-possessed. She was pleased with herself.

'Are you denying you wanted me just now?'

She looked at him levelly, not speaking.

'Liar.'

Lisa stayed cool. 'Sexual attraction can be a powerful drug,' she said judicially. 'Fortunately with me it wears off before I do anything stupid.'

Nikolai was affronted. 'Stupid! How—convenient.'

'A life-saver,' Lisa agreed. She nodded to him briskly, as if they were parting after a business meeting. 'Thanks for the lift home. Goodnight.'

'Not yet,' said Nikolai.

He put a hand on her arm. Her cool shattered into a thousand pieces.

'Let—'

But her words died on her lips at his expression. She stood very still, shaking.

'One question,' said Nikolai. His eyes were chips of dark glass.

'I'm not telling you one thing about Tatiana or—'

'Forget Tatiana,' he said curtly. 'It's not about her.'

'W-well?'

Nikolai sounded furious. 'Who was the man who didn't turn up tonight?'

It was the last thing Lisa had expected. She stared, uncomprehending.

'The empty chair next to you.' He said it as if it was wrenched out of him. 'Who should have been in it?'

Lisa's only answer was a look of contempt. She pulled her arm out of his grip and turned away without a word.

Nikolai took an impetuous step forward. Then stopped, as if he had reined himself in with a force field.

She managed not to run up the front steps, though she wanted to. She felt his eyes on her all the way. His frustration was like a heat source at her back.

Her fingers shook as she inserted her key. She masked the tremor from Nikolai as best she could, opened the door and slipped inside. She did not look back.

Lisa did not have a good day. Sam had already heard about her behaviour at the dinner and lost no time in hitting the roof.

'Look,' he said, shaking a glossy photograph at her. It showed her glaring at Nikolai Ivanov as if he had just given her poison instead of a prestigious award. 'What do you think people are going to think when they see that?'

Lisa shrugged. 'That the man is insufferable?'

Sam almost danced with fury. 'That Napier Kraus bond dealers are a bunch of wild animals, that's what. Do you think clients will want to deal with us when it looks as if you're going to bite them in the fleshy part of the leg as soon as look at them?'

Lisa was angry and tired, and Nikolai Ivanov had caused her a near sleepless night. But Sam spitting over a public relations shot was too good a joke to miss. Against all expectation, she laughed.

He glared at her evilly. 'I've already had Roger Maurice from *Financial Monthly* on the phone, wanting to know if you were always like that. I bet he'll put something in his Rumours column.'

Lisa gave him a cheeky grin. 'Free publicity, Sam.'

He gave a howl. '*Bad* publicity is always free.'

She shrugged again. 'As long as they put in my trading figures as well, it won't be bad,' she said cynically.

'You've got to call him. Apologise.'

Lisa went very still. 'Call who?' she asked, deceptively mild.

'The explorer chap. The guy who handed out the awards.'

'No way,' said Lisa, still mild.

Sam went on as if she hadn't spoken. 'I got a number for him from Maurice.'

He passed a piece of paper across his desk. Lisa looked at it as if it was something disgusting. She did not pick it up.

'I said no.'

'You've got to. He was the Association's guest. And you made him uncomfortable.'

Lisa's eyes narrowed. 'Has he been complaining?'

Sam became evasive. 'Well, if he has, he has justification, doesn't he?'

'*Justification?*' Lisa was outraged.

Sam stabbed a finger down on the unflattering photograph. 'Picture says it all.'

'No, it doesn't. It doesn't say a single thing about *why* I looked like that.'

'Oh, come on, Lisa. Don't play the injured female. If the

guy pinched your bottom, I bet you asked for it. Anyway, you're quite capable of crunching him.'

'He did not,' said Lisa furiously, 'pinch my bottom.'

'Well, then—'

'We'd met before. He was—insulting.'

'Met before?' Sam stared. 'You and Count Ivanov? I don't believe it.'

'Believe what you want.' Lisa was upset, not least because she had said more than she'd meant to. 'Just get this: I'm not—ever—apologising to that man. In fact, I'm not going near him again. And there's nothing you can do to make me. And if you think my showing my midriff to the bond traders of London is going to make one iota of difference to my profit figures, you're more stupid than I thought you were. Now—is that all? I'd like to be back at my desk and do what I'm paid for.'

'Count Ivanov?' Sam was dazed. 'And *you*?'

Lisa gave an elaborate sigh. 'You are such a snob, Sam. We live on the same planet, you know.'

'An East End kid with attitude?'

She flushed. But she managed to shrug. 'Some guys just like slumming, I guess. Now, can I get back to work or is there something else you'd like to shout about?'

Sam choked. 'Get out.'

Lisa sauntered to the door. It was deliberate, designer insolence. It was too much for Sam.

'And get yourself some decent clothes,' he shouted after her.

It followed her out into the dealing room. Several people looked up, intrigued. Lisa flung herself down in front of her screen and concentrated furiously.

She successfully blanked out Sam's complaints. What she could not get rid of was the uncomfortable memory of Nikolai Ivanov. Or—if she was honest—not so much Nikolai as the way she had, just for a moment, responded to him.

He was exactly the sort of man she had learned to mistrust, she thought—superior, arrogant, pleased with himself. The sort of man who thought a girl with no advantages but her brain and her determination was negligible. No—worse. He was the sort of man who thought the only important thing about a girl, any girl, was the way she looked. And the way she responded to him.

So how could she have done just that? Lisa's whole body burned with shame when she thought about it. She had melted in his arms, just as he'd expected her to. He pressed the right buttons and she turned into exactly the sort of stupid, clinging, trembling creature that she most despised. She did not know who she angrier with—Nikolai Ivanov or herself.

She made some savagely profitable deals that afternoon.

'Hey. You drive a hard bargain,' said Rob with admiration, as he peered over her shoulder at her latest.

Lisa showed her teeth to the dealing screen.

'I'll show them I'm no pussy-cat.'

'You are so right,' he agreed fervently.

She had a highly rewarding afternoon. It left her too high to relax. So when she got home she showered and changed, then restlessly opened the French windows and went outside.

The twilight was damp, and smelled of new leaves. A bird she didn't recognise was singing in one of the tall trees. It was almost impossible to believe that her childhood tenement, with its peeling paint, dark, damp walls and pervading smell of the gasworks existed in the same universe. Lisa smiled wryly at the thought.

The communal garden was designed so that each house had its own private plot. These made a densely planted fringe of individual eccentricity, which then gave on to the main sweep of lawn, formal beds and trees. Tatiana had paved her plot, but it was so covered with pots and planters, to say nothing of the climbers clinging to the walls, that it looked like a jungle.

Lisa pushed aside a matted luxuriance of jasmine and

thorny rose branches to reveal a stone trough, green with age. It was filled with heady-scented white hyacinths. She breathed in the scent appreciatively.

'Lisa?'

There was a clatter on the spiral staircase that led down from Tatiana's sitting room. Lisa looked up, peering through the tangle of climbing rose.

'Yes.' It sounded ungracious. She had really wanted to be alone. But this was Tatiana's place, after all. Lisa pulled herself together and tried to be civil. 'I didn't mean to disturb you.'

'You didn't. Hang on.' Tatiana ran down the iron steps, negotiating a tray of seedlings on the way. 'How are you? I haven't seen you for a couple of days.'

'I've had a lot going on,' said Lisa evasively.

Nikolai Ivanov had already occupied too much of her thoughts today. The last thing she wanted was a tête-à-tête with his aunt. She would *not* be tempted to ask her about him, Lisa told herself. Of course she wouldn't. Still, there was no point in testing her resolution to breaking point.

Tatiana peered at her. 'Something wrong?'

Lisa was startled. 'What should be wrong?'

'You look—I don't know—jumpy.'

Lisa grinned. '"Wired" is what we call it in the trade.'

'Working too hard?'

'And winning,' amplified Lisa with satisfaction. 'Achievement is a great buzz. I like to win.'

'You sound like Nicki.'

Lisa tensed. 'Oh?'

'My nephew Nikolai,' Tatiana said innocently. 'The one you met on Sunday. He's quite determined to make me do what he wants.'

'Surprise me,' muttered Lisa.

Tatiana looked mischievous. 'He's so determined to keep an eye on me, he's even taken a flat round here somewhere.'

Lisa just managed not to say that she already knew.

'Creep.'

'Well, I thought it was a bit uncalled for,' Tatiana agreed, hiding a smile. 'I said he ought to come round one evening for a drink and meet you. Just to see that he's making a fuss about nothing.'

Lisa looked at her with blank horror. 'Oh I don't think that would be a good idea at all.'

'But he's got all these terrible ideas about you—'

'I know, and I'll make him sorry.

'What?' said Tatiana, bewildered.

Lisa pulled herself together. 'Tatiana, have you taken that contract I gave you to your solicitor yet?' she said suspiciously.

Tatiana looked shifty.

'Or banked my cheque?'

'I'm spending a lot of time at the studio,' she hedged.

Lisa sighed. 'Listen, I'm with you. I think your nephew Nikolai is an interfering pig. But if you don't get a legal agreement about my tenancy sorted out, he has got a point,' she said with regret. 'For Heaven's sake, get your lawyer to deal with it.'

Tatiana gave in. 'I'll talk to Mr Harrison.'

'Anything. Just get rid of him. *Please*.'

It was heartfelt.

CHAPTER FIVE

LISA hoped that was the end of it. But she had reckoned without the persistence that had carried Tatiana through the creation of several ballets, in spite of the contribution of some highly volatile temperaments. She turned up at the French doors later, bearing a dish of lopsided meringues and a spuriously domestic expression.

It didn't take her long to get down to business, though. 'I don't think you like Nicki.'

Lisa had been going through her wardrobe. It was a depressing business. Now she put down a skirt with a ripped hem and considered her answer.

'I think you could say our feelings are mutual,' she said carefully.

Tatiana looked amused and wise. Lisa found herself seeking desperately for a reason that would satisfy his aunt without actually being slanderous. Rather to her surprise she came up with one. It was even genuine.

'He said I was scruffy.'

She could still hear the tone of amused contempt in which he had said it. And last night he had implied that her appearance was even less respectable than that. But Lisa was not going to waste time thinking about that. It hadn't stopped him wanting to put his hands all over her, had it? She couldn't repress a little shiver at the memory.

'Nikolai has been spoilt,' announced Tatiana. 'All his girlfriends have been fashion plates. He doesn't know it, of course. Although I must say, my dear, you don't seem very *interested* in clothes.'

Lisa gave a choke of laughter and pushed the sad little pile of mending away from her.

'That's what everyone keeps telling me.'

'Then perhaps Nicki was not so wrong, after all. Do you—
er—want to change your wardrobe at all?'

Lisa shrugged. 'No time. No money,' she said succinctly.

Tatiana was all understanding. 'You do need one or the
other,' she agreed. 'Or some first-class advice.' She hesitated.
'I know quite a lot about dressing ballets on a budget,' she
said tentatively.

Lisa was rueful. 'What do you know about turning out City
executives to look like they're dressed in Versace on a
budget?'

'Mmm. Hard one. I'll need to think about it.'

'Do that. Let me know if you find an answer,' Lisa said
lightly.

Tatiana took the hint and left.

By now Lisa had well and truly come down from her high.
There was a new science fiction serial on television and
Tatiana's ethnic cushions were designed for comfort and lazi-
ness. She stretched out luxuriously. She had her bare toes under a tapestry cushion and a plate of hot buttered toast on the
inlaid coffee table beside her when the doorbell rang.

She almost didn't answer. A shadowy monster was lumping
out of the wetlands in pursuit of the inter-galactic detective
and she was on tenterhooks to know what happened next. But
the bell rang again, more insistently. Lisa sighed, kicked aside
the cushion, and ran lightly upstairs.

When she saw who it was, she almost shut the door in his
face.

'Not again,' said Nikolai, with resolution. He inserted himself rapidly into the hallway.

Lisa glared. 'Again?'

'You closed the door on me last night,' he reminded her. 'I
don't like that.'

Lisa looked him up and down. Tonight he was in black
jeans and soft leather jacket. It looked amazingly sexy. She
stayed cool but it was an effort.

'This morning,' she corrected him. 'And I haven't changed my mind.'

'But I have.' He motioned her to precede him downstairs. 'I shouldn't have walked away last night.'

Lisa stood her ground. 'As I remember, I was the one who walked away.'

She worked quite hard not to remember how nearly she had *not* done just that. He looked down into her eyes with an expression that said he could read exactly what she was trying not to remember.

'Only because I let you.'

There was a small silence. Lisa allowed herself to look him up and down a second time. Slowly and deliberately. And to give half a smile, as if she was not very impressed. Almost, she thought savagely, as if she too had had the benefit of centuries of aristocratic breeding and education.

'Another unreconstructed male to add to my collection,' she drawled at last.

He raised an eyebrow.

Goaded, she heard her voice go up. 'You're not a new experience, believe me.'

Nikolai's eyes gleamed. 'No?'

He swooped. She found her legs scooped from under her as he hoisted her up against his chest. Lisa lost her cool. To her everlasting shame she gave a screech of pure panic, and clutched at his jacket as he made for the stairs.

'What are you *doing*?'

He narrowed his eyes as he looked down at her.

'Unreconstructed male-type things.'

He started down the stairs. The drop to the bottom looked like the north face of the Eiger. Lisa transferred her eyes rapidly to the shoulder of his jacket and hung on.

'You're mad,' she said with conviction.

But she didn't move a muscle until he had successfully descended the entire flight. Then she made a leap for freedom. It was neither graceful nor easy, but it was effective. Lisa fell to one knee. Nikolai held out a hand. She ignored it, staggering to her feet.

He cocked his head to the sound of the television.

'You're not alone?'

Lisa nearly lied. But in an instant she realised that Nikolai would only march into the sitting room to check.

She got to her feet and said bitterly, 'From now on I'll make sure I have a party every night.'

Nikolai's eyes flickered. 'Then we'd better get our business finished now.'

'What business?'

Just as she had thought: without bothering to answer he walked past her into the sitting room. As if he owned it, she thought, fulminating.

For a moment she hesitated. But, however dubious his morals, she didn't think Nikolai Ivanov would offer her violence with his great-aunt pottering about above their heads. So she shrugged and followed.

He turned off the television and looked at the coffee table, with its plate of half-eaten toast and warm mug of hot chocolate. There was a curious expression on his face.

'Very innocent. I would never have had you down as a nursery food addict.'

Lisa exploded. 'Nursery food! There speaks a man who was brought up by nanny behind a green baize door.'

Nikolai was taken aback. 'What?'

'Oh, forget it.'

She scooped up the plate and mug protectively and took them into the tiny kitchen. He didn't let her go alone.

'Explain,' he ordered.

'I said forget it.' She turned and faced him. '*Count* Ivanov.'

Nikolai went still. 'Count—? You mean you're an unreconstructed inverted snob!' he taunted.

Lisa turned away, annoyed with herself. 'Tell me what this business of yours is,' she said curtly. 'Then get out.'

Nikolai propped himself against the door lintel, blocking her exit. 'Are you really not curious?'

'Wild with it,' Lisa said, deadpan. 'So tell me. What do you want?'

He smiled a slow, lazy tiger's smile.

'I mean curious about what would have happened last night. If we had stayed together.'

The implications of it hung in the air between them. Not articulated, sure, but *there*, deliberate and unmistakable. If she closed her eyes she could feel it, almost as if it had happened: his breath on her skin, their bodies entwined, falling...

As he no doubt intended. Lisa had a moment of near panic. What sort of idiot did he think she was?

She pushed past him into the sitting room. She had to put more distance between them or he would see exactly how strongly he had got to her. She went to the window, ensuring that there was a substantial armchair between them.

She was furious with herself, but she couldn't help it. He was just too big, too powerful. Telling herself she could handle it, she folded her arms and gave him a wide, false smile.

'That usually works, does it?' she asked affably.

He didn't like that. He had swung round, following her until she retreated behind her chair. Now he stopped. The predatory smile died too.

'Excuse me?'

'The whole box of tricks. Sexy eyes. Husky voice. General innuendo,' she explained helpfully. 'Do you find it delivers the goods?'

Nikolai's brows twitched together in a black frown. 'What goods?'

'Well, in this case, I suppose, me.'

He didn't deny it. He was silent for a moment. Then said in an annoyed voice, 'You are very blunt.'

'That's me,' Lisa agreed. 'Call a spade a shovel, I do. Always have.'

Nikolai stared at her as if she was a new sort of animal he had never seen before.

'Not very romantic,' he said at last.

Lisa raised her eyebrows. 'What's romantic about telling

me I passed up a good thing just because I didn't want to sleep with you last night?'

To her surprise he flushed slightly. 'I never said that.'

'No. But wasn't that what I was supposed to think?' Lisa demanded shrewdly.

'*Very* blunt.'

'My mother always told me to tell the truth and shame the devil.'

He was torn between annoyance and reluctant amusement.

'Which casts me as the devil, I suppose?'

Lisa shrugged.

Nikolai had had an instructive couple of days. He had not yet met Alec Palmer who, rumour said, was her discarded lover, but everyone else had told the same story about Lisa Romaine. She was sharp and ambitious and was not going to let anything get in the way of her ambition. Depending on whether they liked her, people either said she was impetuous and temperamental, or she was steady as a rock.

Her boss, clearly not an admirer, had said she would pick a fight as soon as look at you. Nikolai was beginning to see what he meant.

Irritated, he said now, 'It would be more sensible to conciliate me, you know.'

Lisa pursed her mouth. 'Conciliate? Is that a fancy way of saying I ought to go to bed with you?'

He was angry now. 'Do you have to be so crass?'

Lisa relaxed. Anger was easier to deal with than that prowling sexuality. She smiled.

'Don't like the truth, Count Ivanov?'

He controlled himself. 'I don't like being accused of trying to blackmail a woman into bed.'

Lisa nodded. 'I can understand that,' she said with spurious sympathy. 'Just like I don't care for it when people try to manipulate me.'

Their eyes met with the clash of steel on steel. There was an electric silence. Nikolai drew a long breath.

'What are we fighting for?' he said at last. His voice was strained.

'You're the one who forced your way into my home. You tell me.'

He sighed. 'Come on, Lisa. It doesn't have to be like this.'

'You've made it very clear what you think it should be like,' Lisa said grimly. 'I'm not interested.'

Nikolai's eyes flashed suddenly. 'You mean you'd be happier to pretend you're not interested in what we could be like together.'

Lisa's head went back as if he had hit her.

Nikolai took no notice. He swept on. 'And you want me to pretend too.'

Lisa found her voice. 'That's crazy.'

'Is it?'

He sat down on the arm of an elderly chintz-covered chair. It had been left in the flat by Tatiana, and he leaned against its frayed back with the familiarity of one who had done the same thing many times before. It gave Lisa an odd feeling that she was the invader, not him.

He swung a foot and surveyed her calmly. 'Do you know what I do?' he asked idly.

Lisa blinked. 'I thought you were a modern-day Tarzan,' she said nastily.

'Animal behaviourist.' He gave her a deeply untrustworthy smile. 'I study body language.'

Lisa leaped about a foot in the air and speedily unclasped her folded arms. Nikolai's smile widened.

'Too late.'

Since that was exactly what she'd been thinking herself, Lisa was irritated.

'I am not an animal,' she said unwisely.

He laughed aloud at that.

'Shall I tell you what your body language tells me?' he said conversationally.

'No.'

He ignored that. 'Dominant female. Doesn't confide.

Doesn't depend on other members of the pack. Quick to aggression. Sexually—'

Lisa choked.

He smiled and went on. 'Sexually uninterested, on the whole.'

She was surprised into an unwise exclamation. 'But I thought you said—'

'I said *on the whole*,' Nikolai repeated gently. 'For example: take the awards dinner. Better still, take that loud club you like so much. In both places there were plenty of men making courtship gestures to you. Some more subtle than others.' He frowned momentarily. 'In fact in the club there were a couple who were all over you. You didn't seem to notice. Not a flicker of response.'

Lisa was triumphant. 'I *told* you—'

'But you noticed me,' he finished softly.

Lisa felt as if she had walked into a wall. It was true! She stared at him, appalled. She couldn't think of a thing to say.

'Which is why I'm not going to help you tell lies about it. Especially to yourself. It is not,' he added with odious kindness, 'good for you.'

'Why, thank you so much,' said Lisa. Her scorn was slightly shaky, but at least it felt as if she was fighting back.

'Honesty is always best. You probably don't feel very pleased with me now—'

'No!' exclaimed Lisa, her scorn improving.

'—but you'll thank me in the end.'

'I'll bear that in mind,' she said drily. 'If I ever get round to thinking about you again, that is.'

He shook his head. 'Quick to aggression,' he reminded her wickedly.

Lisa curbed herself. It was an effort.

'An interesting diagnosis,' she said without expression. 'Based on so much evidence too.'

He grinned. 'I'm a trained observer.'

'Well, I don't want you observing me,' Lisa retorted. 'In fact, I don't want you here at all. So will you go now, please?'

Nikolai did not move. 'We have a number of things to discuss first.'

Lisa's chin jutted dangerously. 'Such as?'

'The terms of your agreement with Tatiana.'

She stared at him blankly.

'You have got a formal agreement with Tatiana?' he asked patiently.

Lisa's temper began to strain at the leash. 'That's her business,' she said curtly. 'If you want to discuss your aunt's affairs, talk to her.'

'I've tried,' he admitted.

'Then try again. Don't think you can weasel details out of me.'

She advanced on him, green eyes bright. Not with warmth. Nikolai stood up.

'All I want—'

'If Tatiana has told you to get lost, I'm with Tatiana,' Lisa said with feeling. 'Out. Now.'

'I have a right to protect my family,' said Nikolai, suddenly as angry as she.

'Then go protect them. But don't expect me to spy on Tatiana or anyone else. I'm not a sneak.'

'No. You're a clever piece with a good line in hard-luck stories,' he told her.

All the lazy amusement had fallen away, and he was suddenly icy with rage. It shocked Lisa, though she congratulated herself on how right she had been not to trust him when he was smiling.

Just like Terry, she thought. And then shut the thought down at once. Nikolai Ivanov was arrogant and insulting and he would answer for it. He did not need to answer for Terry's heartlessness as well.

She snapped her fingers in mock forgetfulness. 'Didn't somebody say something about being conciliating?'

Nikolai stampeded over that. 'Don't forget I've seen you on your own territory. You don't look like a victim to me.'

In pure instinct, he put his hands on her shoulders. He didn't know himself what he intended to do. To hold her still while he made her listen to him, maybe.

Certainly he didn't mean to frighten her. He would not have believed that he could. Or that any man could. So he was utterly unprepared for what happened next.

One moment he was glaring at her, holding her at arm's length; there was a split second when something wild leaped in Lisa's green eyes, and then she hauled away from him as if she had been scalded. Off balance and startled, Nikolai staggered. The rucked rug completed his downfall. Lisa did not break his fall.

'No,' said Lisa, breathing hard. 'I'm not a victim.'

Nikolai sat on the Kelim rug and shook his head carefully. 'What was that for? Did you think I was going to hurt you?'

He looked up at her, annoyed. That was when he saw the expression in her eyes. His annoyance died.

'You *did*,' he said, on a note of discovery.

Lisa was more shaken than she was willing to admit. Her own violent reaction had shocked her. What was there about this man that his every touch seemed to set off all her warning signals? She retreated behind the sofa as he got to his feet. Not because she was afraid of him. But because her every instinct was to hold out a hand to help him, and she didn't want to risk another surge of unwanted electricity at his touch.

Panting a little, she said, 'If I were the sort of woman you think I am, I'd go straight upstairs and tell Tatiana about this conversation.'

His eyes hooded themselves. He didn't say anything for a moment. Then, 'And?'

'I'm not going to. Not because I'm afraid of you.' She let her eyes skim over him with disgust. 'But because I like Tatiana and she's obviously fond of you. I don't want to be the one to shatter her illusions. So get out. And don't come back.'

There was a long, long silence. Lisa could hear her own breathing. It sounded as if she had run up a hill.

Then, without a word, he turned and left.

*   *   *

Nikolai met Alec Palmer in a City wine bar. It was in the basement of a concrete building but there was sawdust on the floor and men were drinking beer out of copper tankards.

'Lisa won't come here,' Alec said. 'These days she says it's too phoney.'

Privately Nikolai agreed. He didn't say so.

'So she won't interrupt us by chance. Useful,' he observed. He ordered a platter of sandwiches and took a bottle of champagne over to a secluded corner. 'So what can you tell me about this woman?' he said, pouring wine into Alec's glass.

Alec didn't need to be asked a second time. He was still smarting from his last encounter with Lisa. In a ten-minute diatribe Nikolai heard that she was hard and shallow and used people ruthlessly.

'She's on the make,' concluded Alec simply.

It was only what Nikolai had thought himself. So what demon of perversity made him protest?

'There's nothing wrong with trying to improve your life,' he said temperately.

Alec's mouth set in a bitter line. 'Improve, huh! That wasn't hard. She comes from the bottom of the pile, did you know that?'

The man's spite was blatant.

Nikolai tried to sound neutral. 'No, I didn't.'

'When I first knew Lisa Romaine she was an East End kid who thought fish and chips was the treat of a lifetime. Now she lives on sushi and champagne. But is she satisfied? Is she hell!'

'Maybe she just wants to experience new things.'

'Sure. New man, new rung up the ladder. Every move she makes, she gets rid of the last lot of friends. They say that was how she got her start in the first place.'

Nikolai sat very still. 'Sleeping with the boss?' he queried. Every bone in his body rejected it.

Alec shrugged. 'That's the word. I wasn't in the City at the time, so of course I don't know. I do know that everyone in the house said it would be curtains for us when she was promoted. Acton wasn't smart enough. *I* wasn't smart enough.'

Nikolai winced. It all sounded horribly plausible. Indeed, it sounded exactly what his grandfather had already worked out, alerted to the situation by Tatiana's conscientious accountant. And everything Lisa herself had said to him since they met tended to confirm it. Only...

'She seems so honest,' he said, almost to himself. Alec looked up sharply. He gave a harsh laugh.

'You, too, huh?'

Nikolai stared at him, disconcerted.

'It gets us all that way, mate. You look at the big green eyes and the tatty clothes and you think—there's something special here, and I'm the only one to see it.'

His hurt was as blatant as the spite. Nikolai looked away. Anything that painful should have stayed private.

'Only you're not,' Alec said, brooding. 'We've all been there. See Lisa. Want Lisa. Take her another rung up the ladder. Say goodbye, Lisa.' The look he gave the tall man in the exquisitely cut suit was malicious. 'Welcome to the club.'

'I do not,' said Nikolai between his teeth, 'want Lisa Romaine.'

He was not talking to Alec.

Lisa didn't normally go to see her mother and sister more than once a week. But Kit worried her. So she slipped away from the nightly meeting as soon as she could on Thursday evening and took the train to their suburb.

Joanne greeted her with relief.

'She hasn't been to work for three days,' she said in despair. 'I don't think she's eaten a thing either. Talk to her.'

Kit was sitting on her bedroom floor again. She had closed the curtains and the room was lit only by candles. This time the music was some strange plain chant.

Kit looked up when Lisa opened the door and gave a wan smile.

'Mother called in the cavalry, then.'

Lisa responded to the smile rather than the words. She came in, closing the door carefully, and slid down on the floor beside her sister.

All the cushions were piled up round Kit, as if she had dug herself in for a siege. But she passed Lisa a large toy alligator to put behind her back. Lisa recognised it. She had brought it back as a silly present for Kit when she went to a conference in New Orleans. For some reason it moved Lisa unbearably.

'Oh, lamb,' she said, her voice breaking.

Kit dropped her head on Lisa's shoulder.

'Mum thinks I'm losing the plot again, doesn't she? She keeps making me soup. I can't bear it,' she said with the calm of absolute despair. 'I know I have to eat. I *do*. But when Mum starts getting at me all I want to do is sleep.'

Lisa put her arm round the thin shoulders.

'Lee, I'm scared.' Kit sounded it.

'This can't go on. There has to be an answer. I'll find one,' Lisa promised in a low voice. 'I *will*.'

She spent every hour she wasn't working on the telephone the next day. It was no use. Kit had tried too many treatments already.

'I don't care what it costs,' Lisa said desperately.

'Ms Romaine, Kit has done every course we can offer her,' said her consultant's secretary wearily. 'She just doesn't want to get better. There is nothing anyone can do.'

Lisa banged her fist on the desk. 'But—'

There was an ominous splitting sound.

'Your jacket's gone,' murmured Angela.

Sam's secretary was passing with a plastic tray full of cups of coffee from the machine. She left a coffee and helpfully fingered a rip below the collar.

'I'll talk to Mr Feldstein and get back to you,' said the telephone.

'Thank you for nothing,' said Lisa to the disconnected line. She took off her jacket and looked at it moodily. Angela was right. What was worse, Lisa suspected the jacket was beyond repair. It had split down the central seam.

'Oh, wonderful! Even fate is determined to make me buy some new clothes.'

'Great,' said one of the other girls. 'Lie back and enjoy it.'

Lisa sighed. 'I hate shopping.'

She didn't say that now Kit was ill again she didn't want to spend money on anything until she knew how much she would need to cover the next lot of therapy. But Angela was a friend, and knew what she must be thinking.

Passing back to her office from Sam's conference, she bent and murmured in Lisa's ear, 'Cheer up. You're living in the right place for cheap clothes. The Portobello Market doesn't just sell antiques to rich tourists, you know.'

So Saturday morning found Lisa threading her away through the multilingual crowds in the famous street market. The stalls were so close together that they completely cut off the brilliant spring sunshine from the pavement. What was more, by the time people stopped to examine the traders' wares, and to bargain, there was just about room for the crowd to move in single file. It went at a snail's pace. Lisa gave up and moved out into the road.

She rapidly left behind the stalls selling silver, porcelain, books, bric-à-brac, and even Thirties fashion, full of beading and crushed velvets. Briefly sidetracked, Lisa fingered cocktail pyjamas in black and gold silk wistfully. They fascinated her. She had to work hard to remind herself that she had no money to play with and ought to move on.

The further north she went, she found, the more utilitarian the goods became. First fruit and vegetables, then cheap sheets and bolts of material, then second-hand furniture and odds and ends that not even their optimistic vendors could call antique. This was more like the street markets of her childhood, she thought. Joanne had furnished their dingy flat and kept them fed and clothed from stalls like this. In spite of the sunshine, Lisa shivered.

She prowled among the stalls. There were racks of clothes,

all right, but nothing she could wear to work. The poor cut of the jackets showed the moment she tried any of them on. And the skirts were made of synthetic materials that screamed how cheap they were. Even Lisa, who was outraged by the price of the designer clothes her female colleagues wore, couldn't convince herself that anything here would do.

Sighing, she retraced her steps. But by now the morning was advanced and the tourists were out in force. And so were the sharks. Once she thought she felt a hand feeling for her pocket, and grinned. No pickpocket would get anything from her. One advantage of being familiar with street markets was that you knew you had to guard your money. Lisa's was in a waist-pouch, tucked securely under her sweater.

The closer she got to the antiques, the denser the crowd. Lisa found herself jostled from road to pavement and back again. Nearly everyone was taller than her and, looking up at the passers-by, she had a strange, frightening feeling that she was sinking below waves of people.

And then she stumbled...

The tall man who had been shadowing her at a discreet distance began to race forward, pushing affronted pedestrians out of the way.

Lisa almost recovered her balance. But then a distracted woman talking into her mobile phone lurched into her and she began to fall. She cried out. But no one heard her. She flung up an arm to protect her eyes and curled into a protective ball as she fell.

Nikolai flung himself on his knees beside her. He leaned over, shielding her with his body. Lisa opened her eyes.

'You!'

Nikolai looked down. 'Are you hurt?'

Lisa shook her head shakily. 'I—I don't think so.'

But when she tried to stand her head swam, and she had to grab at the nearest support. It turned out to be Nikolai Ivanov, but she was beyond caring. He straightened, holding her almost tenderly. Lisa found she was clinging to his hand.

Nikolai shouldered open a space in the throng. Still clinging, Lisa let herself be led through.

'Thank you,' she said in a subdued voice.

'Are you sure you're all right? You're very pale.'

'I'm fine.' But she swayed.

He caught her.

'We'll go back to my place. It's nearer.'

Lisa put a hand to her swimming head. She hardly heard him. After one swift look at her chalk-white face, Nikolai clamped her strongly to his side and surged through the crowd. By the time they reached the building where he had rented his flat, he was half carrying her.

The dazzling sun, the crowds, the anxiety of the last days were all taking a sudden and alarming toll. Lisa leaned against him, her senses swimming.

Nikolai never once let go of her. On the doorstep, in the lift, while he was feeling for the key and unlocking the unfamiliar door—the whole time she felt as if his arms surrounded her. He was like a rock. And once they were inside the dark flat he let the door fall shut and swung her up into his arms.

It was so different from the night at her flat. This time he carried her as if she were fragile and precious. Lisa felt his heart beating slow and steady under her cheek. She closed her eyes and gave herself up to the utter luxury of feeling protected.

Nikolai brought her a glass of water and hunkered down beside the sofa. Lisa opened her eyes. For the first time since she had known him, she thought, he was looking at her without suspicion. Lisa could hardly believe the change.

'Thank you.' She took the glass and sipped.

'What happened?'

He was so close. If she swayed just a couple of inches she could lean against his chest. If she did, she was almost certain that he would put his arm round her. She wanted it so badly it was a physical pain.

Stop it. You can't afford to go leaning on a man. Especially not this man.

She drank the water quickly.

Nikolai was frowning. 'Can't you remember what happened? Do you think you could have hit your head?'

'No.' Lisa shook her head. 'I lost my footing, that's all. I wasn't hurt.'

He was dissatisfied. 'I don't buy that. You looked like a ghost. And normal healthy people don't just lose their footing like that.'

Lisa bit her lip. 'It was the crowd,' she admitted at last. 'I felt as if I was drowning. I know it was silly.'

'Not so silly.' He touched her cheek fleetingly. 'You're only a little thing, aren't you?'

There was a caressing note in his voice. It made her want... It made her want a lot of silly things, Lisa told herself firmly. Things she would not have dreamed of if she hadn't still been a bit shaky from the fall.

She gave him back the glass and swung her legs off the sofa. And incidentally moved further away from him.

'I'm better now.'

Nikolai noted the distance she put between them, his eyes shrewd.

'You don't look it,' he told her frankly. 'At least sit for a moment. Get your breath back.'

To tell the truth, Lisa was glad to comply. Maybe it was his proximity, but her heart was pounding uncomfortably hard. She nodded.

Nikolai stood up. 'What were you doing in Portobello Market? Are you a collector?'

Lisa looked up. The brown eyes had gone opaque and suspicious again. For a moment she felt almost bereft.

She pulled herself together and answered quickly, 'No, I was looking for clothes.'

Too quickly to consider her words. She had told the truth and it made no sense to Nikolai.

'Clothes?' He grappled with it. 'You mean antique dresses or something?'

Lisa stiffened. 'No.'

He was blank. 'But nobody buys their clothes from a market stall.'

'That just shows how hidebound you are,' said Lisa with returning hostility. 'Lots of people have no alternative. It depends on their disposable income.'

'And yours must be hefty,' he pointed out, with some justice. 'You must be able to afford any clothes you want, starting with the Paris boutiques.'

Lisa bristled. 'You don't know a thing about me.'

'I know what bond dealers earn,' said Nikolai unanswerably. 'The more successful they are, the bigger their bonuses—isn't that right? And only this week I gave you an award for being the top cat in London.' He shrugged. 'So—I find it difficult to believe you're so hard up you have to buy your clothes off a barrow.'

Lisa flushed.

'Unless you're spending a fortune on something else, of course.' His eyes narrowed suddenly. 'Have you got a drug problem?'

She forgot she was feeling frail. She bounced off the sofa in outrage.

'Of course I haven't.'

'Then where does the money go?'

'What business is it of yours?'

He was no longer kind. In fact he didn't look the same man as he had been five minutes ago. His eyes were as hard as stone.

'Tatiana trusts you,' he said levelly. 'It's up to me to make sure that trust is not betrayed.'

'*Oh!*'

They were back right where they had started, thought Lisa. She must be more shaken than she'd thought, because quite suddenly she couldn't bear it. She gave in and told him the truth.

'I support my mother and sister,' she said quietly. 'They're not extravagant. But bond dealing is a young man's game, and I don't know how long I'll earn at my present rate. So I'm buying their house on a very short mortgage. That's where most of the money goes.'

She sat back among the cushions as if she had run a five-mile race. It felt like a defeat.

Nikolai was silent.

Then, to her astonishment, he said slowly, 'You sound as if you aren't keen on being a bond dealer. Don't you enjoy it?'

Lisa hesitated. But telling the truth seemed to be unavoidable this morning.

'I'm good at it. I like doing something I'm good at. And, of course, it pays the bills. Or at least—' She broke off.

Nikolai waited. But she didn't go on.

'You're a woman of secrets, Lisa Romaine.'

Involuntarily she imagined what it would be like if this man knew all her secrets. He would not, she thought, hesitate to use them against her. She had a brief vision of him standing in Joanne's small crowded sitting room, looking all the way down his Roman nose at Kit and her mother. Lisa shivered.

'I hope so,' she said with feeling.

He frowned. 'You're not very trusting, are you?'

'Makes two of us,' she retorted.

Nikolai was taken aback. *'Touché,'* he said after a moment. 'Look. I'll make a deal with you.'

'What sort of deal?' Lisa was suspicious again.

'Don't look like that,' he said involuntarily. 'I'm not asking you to sell your soul. Or even your body,' he added, as her frown did not lighten.

Lisa glared, refusing to blush. 'Makes a nice change.'

'No, it doesn't. Bodies are for giving, not selling.' He touched her cheek briefly. 'And I live in hope.' Before she could speak, or even react by a gesture, he swept on, 'But for the moment I'm only interested in Tatiana. Right?'

Lisa's eyes fell. 'Well?' she said gruffly.

'I won't try to stop Tatiana renting the garden flat to you. I won't interfere in any way. And in return—'

'Yes?'

He hesitated. 'I'd like to call you from time to time.'

Her head reared up. 'But you said—'

'Not about us. About Tatiana. She isn't getting any younger. And there's no family member in London for her to turn to if she has a problem. You, on the other hand, are going to be just downstairs.'

Lisa stared at him blankly.

'You want me to spy on Tatiana?'

He pursed his lips. 'Shall we say, keep a friendly eye on her?'

'But—me? You don't trust me.'

'My feelings about you,' said Nikolai carefully, 'are best described as mixed.'

'Well, then—'

'A weekly call,' he said softly, 'will keep an eye on you as well. Don't you see?'

There was a long, complicated silence.

'I think this is another one of your devious plans,' Lisa said slowly.

Nikolai gave her a bland smile. 'That's your privilege. Is it a deal?'

There was no reason for it, but all of a sudden it felt like the riskiest thing she had ever done in her life. And his enigmatic expression only increased her wariness. Lisa told herself not to be a fool. She drew a shaky breath.

'Deal.'

CHAPTER SIX

'RIGHT,' said Nikolai. He stood up, and said in quite another tone, 'Now we can start again.'

He held out a hand. Lisa looked up at him, confused. He seized her own hand and shook it vigorously.

'Nikolai Ivanov. How do you do?'

She seized her hand back. 'More games,' she said scornfully.

'What's wrong with games? Don't you play, Lisa Romaine?'

'Not with you,' said Lisa. It was heartfelt.

He gave a soft laugh. 'I'll take that as a compliment.'

She stood up. 'Take it any way you like.'

She looked round for her waist-pouch. Nikolai didn't help. Instead he leaned against the crowded mantelpiece and watched with mild interest.

'You know, you're not at all like your advance publicity,' he informed her.

Lisa didn't answer. She picked a pile of books off a table and lifted some papers. Her bag wasn't there.

'Your boss, now. He thinks you're a real party girl.'

That stopped her dead in her tracks. 'My boss?'

'I don't remember his name. He thinks your skirts are too short.'

'He thinks I should be a man,' said Lisa curtly, resuming her search.

'Also, your tops are too tight and your jewellery is naff.' His eyes danced. 'I'm guessing, but I'd say he doesn't know about the tattoo?'

Lisa stopped looking and turned to face him, hands on hips.

115

'OK. Where is my bag?'

He looked reproachful. 'Don't you even want to know where I met your boss? Or why?'

'It's obvious you were spying on me,' said Lisa, with patience. She didn't sound as if she cared one way or the other. Which was rather impressive as she was seething inwardly. 'I hope you had a good time.'

'Very instructive. I particularly like that big swivel seat that goes up and down. Is that a perk of being a manager, or do you need it to see over the top of the screens?'

Lisa went cold. He had been in the dealing room. He had come in and watched her work and she had had no idea he was there. She could not have felt more exposed if he had filmed her in her bedroom.

'You take your spying seriously,' she said, when she could speak.

'"Get your hands off her, Rob, you pathetic lecher,"' he quoted softly.

Lisa's head reared up. 'You were there *then*?'

Nikolai didn't answer that directly. 'And you don't need a man.'

Lisa remembered that she had shouted that at Rob when he'd offered to escort her to the awards dinner. She fought rising colour.

'Where were you?' she said thinly. 'I didn't see you.'

'I was with your boss. It was you who left me your business card, after all.' He shrugged. 'I checked. He invited me in. As I say, it was instructive.'

'I'm glad,' said Lisa. It was a lie. 'Now, please will you give me my waist-pouch? I've got a lot to do this morning and I'd like to get on.'

Nikolai didn't move from the mantelpiece. 'And is it true?'

'Of course it—' Lisa checked. 'Is what true?'

'Do you really not need a man?' he reminded her.

'Oh, puh-lease!' She was exasperated.

'Because you told me that you lived with one man at a

time. And there doesn't seem to be anyone else living in Tatiana's basement at the moment.'

He watched her closely. He was not going to tell her that he had met Alec Palmer. Not yet, anyway. He wanted her to tell him about Alec herself. He wanted there to be a reason for the break-up that was more than her upwardly mobile career. He waited.

Lisa looked at him with hot eyes. 'My bag.'

Nikolai's shoulders slumped.

'Your boss is wrong, isn't he?' he said slowly.

'My *bag*.'

'You're not a party girl at all. Though for your own reasons you choose to pretend you are. You're a career woman going places. And nothing is more important than that.'

'Well, at least it's better than hanging around snooping on people,' Lisa snapped, goaded. 'You obviously don't have any career at all.'

Nikolai was taken aback. It hadn't occurred to him that she would turn his own arguments against him. He had no defence prepared.

Lisa was in a rage. 'Why bother with the explorer bit?' she said with contempt. 'Or is it a rich man's hobby to take you somewhere warm in winter?'

His eyes narrowed. 'What makes you think I'm rich?'

She shrugged.

'Did you ask?'

'Why shouldn't I? Are you the only one allowed to check up on other people?' she flashed.

'I wasn't asking about your wealth.'

'Yes, you were. Along with a whole load of other things.' She gave him a nasty smile. 'I'm just not as nosy as you. I don't *care* how many girlfriends you have.'

She spied her waist-pouch. It must have fallen off when he'd carried her in. It was lying half hidden under the sofa. She caught it up with a cry of triumph.

'Now,' she said, running impatient fingers through her hair, 'I'm going. I'll keep my part of the bargain because

I'm fond of Tatiana, and I think you probably are too. But that's all. No more spying. No more little talks. Right?'

Nikolai was white with rage. 'Right,' he snarled.

Lisa spent an unsatisfactory weekend. She tidied the flat, read the end of week forecasts that the economists delivered on Friday afternoons, did some alternative projections, tried to relax. It was no use. Every time she looked up from her work, every time she closed the door on a newly tidied cupboard, she saw Nikolai Ivanov's face.

'It's just because he made me mad,' Lisa said to the bathroom mirror.

But it wasn't, and she knew it. Plenty of men made her mad. She didn't see Alec Palmer's face every time she closed her eyes. Even Terry Long, who had done a number on her which at one time she'd thought was terminal, hadn't haunted her like this.

But Nikolai was different. He had got under her skin, with that arrogance, that mockery—and that terrifyingly seductive attention. He had a way of listening to you as if what you were saying was the most significant thing he had ever heard.

'Marketing,' said Lisa loudly.

She knew about marketing. Terry had told her she was a marvel, the real thing, an original talent. And the fact that she came from a poor background with minimal education only made her instincts for business more acute. He had called her his little savage. But when he'd taken her to bed she had been his lamb.

Lisa closed her eyes, wincing. OK, she had been eighteen and in love, but there was still no excuse for being quite such an idiot. When he'd been offered the New York job she'd found out what he'd really thought.

'Oh, come on, Lisa. You knew it was just a bit of fun,' he had said, with that wide false smile she had come to hate.

Lisa didn't know what to say. Her silence irritated Terry.

'You didn't think I was going to *marry* you?' He gave a loud laugh.

'You said we were alike,' she said, bewildered. She still didn't understand what was happening. 'You said you admired me.'

Terry was impatient with this naivety.

'Of course I did. Any man would. You didn't have to take it as gospel.'

'So you were just pretending?'

'The working class is so literal-minded,' he complained. 'I was marketing, darling. Marketing.'

Lisa looked at him and realised that she had never seen the real man before, though she had slept in his arms night after night for months and thought she could rely on him for ever.

She said slowly, 'Do you even like me?'

'Not when you're being difficult,' Terry admitted, with unusual honesty.

That was when Lisa began to fight back. Her chin came up in a characteristic gesture.

'So why have you been wasting your time?'

'You're fun,' he said simply.

'I see.' Lisa's tone was dry. 'Trash, but fun.'

He grinned. 'Tough, too.' He meant it as a compliment.

Lisa determined from that moment that she would be tough indeed. It seemed the only way to survive.

It didn't change her radically. She still liked men. She went out with them. But she made sure that her heart stayed detached.

And she had been happy with the way she ran her life. She refused to commit herself but she had her own code and honoured it. In a relationship she was tender, passionate and fun. When it was over, she was scrupulous. It had seemed a good way to live.

Until Nikolai Ivanov had stormed into her life with his unflattering assumptions and his sexy eyes. And made her

question everything she'd thought she'd had sorted out for
years. Not least what she wanted herself.

Do you really not need a man? The husky voice rever-
berated around in her memory, mocking her.

'*Damn,*' said Lisa.

And stamped out to seek comfort from her friends.

Nikolai rang his grandfather.

'I'm staying on,' he said curtly.

Pauli's heart sank. He had half expected this. 'The Borneo
expedition?'

'Good heavens, no. There's some mystery about the
woman who is living with Tatiana.' His rage had cooled,
but it had left him all the more determined. 'I'm not leaving
London until I find out what it is.'

'Oh.' Pauli digested this. 'But you said yesterday that
Harrison was satisfied she'd behaved properly over the tenancy agreement.'

Nikolai snorted. 'She's too clever to do anything illegal.'

There was a brief silence. Then Pauli said, 'Nicki, are
you sure you aren't getting this out of proportion? I mean,
in the end it's Tatiana's business who she takes into her
house.'

'I finish what I start,' said Nikolai.

His grandfather said slowly, 'This isn't just to prove a
point, is it?'

'What point?' said Nikolai, impatient.

'That all women respond if you take a firm line with
them.'

For a moment Nikolai was speechless. Then he remembered their conversation at the wedding.

'You have a thoroughly inconvenient memory,' he told
his grandfather. 'And I wouldn't put money on the chances
of any man taking a firm line with Lisa Romaine.'

'Oh?' His grandfather sounded a lot more cheerful all of
a sudden. 'She sounds interesting. Perhaps Tatiana would

bring her to visit if we asked. Your grandmother would like to meet her.'

Nikolai was no fool. 'Don't even think about it,' he warned his grandfather softly. 'My girl. My fight. Stay out of it.'

The sun came out in a blaze of early summer. It turned the garden beyond Lisa's window into a green tapestry. The warmth nearly lured her away from the necessary task of reviewing her wardrobe. But Lisa was firm with herself.

The situation was desperate. Consulted about the ripped jacket, even Lisa's mother had had to admit it was beyond repair. Which left Lisa with only one business jacket of any description and no summer clothes she could wear to work at all.

Nikolai Ivanov was right. She was scruffy. Other people had said the same thing, of course. But for some reason it was Nikolai's contempt that she remembered. And it hurt.

She climbed into frayed shorts and a tee shirt and took a mug of coffee out into the sunshine. She reviewed her options, frowning. There were other people in the gardens today, but no one disturbed her as she sat on the damp grass, her back against the trunk of a copper beech.

Or no one except Tatiana. She came up wearing ragged cotton dungarees and, if Lisa was any judge, several hundred pounds' worth of silk headscarf to keep the twigs off her hair.

'You look preoccupied. What's the matter?'

Lisa told her. In detail.

'Ah,' said Tatiana. 'I've been thinking about that. Do you use charity shops?'

Lisa pulled a face. 'I hoped I'd got past that. My mother used to get everything there when we were children.'

'There are charities and charities,' said Tatiana professionally. 'Go to one in a smart area, where the cocktail party classes are throwing out things they've worn a couple of times, and you can get some very nice stuff indeed. Especially if you're as slim as you are.'

'Where do I find the smart areas, then?'

Tatiana smiled at her innocence. 'Here. Holland Park. Kensington. Chelsea—there are several if you wander down the King's Road.'

'Sounds like hard work,' said Lisa morosely.

But Tatiana refused to repress her enthusiasm. 'It will be fun. I'll just wash the dirt off my hands and we'll get going.'

Lisa threw up her hands, laughing. 'Anything you say, *madame*. I just need to call my family first. I may need to go home.'

But Joanne was adamant that Kit was best left alone. Mr Feldstein had telephoned and so had someone from the local self-help group. Kit had eaten some rice and a few vegetables and then gone out to a movie with a couple from the group.

'But she still feels guilty about your presentation,' finished Joanne. 'Don't come home and remind her that she let you down.'

So Lisa had no excuse not to go shopping.

In the end she found she enjoyed it. She had never really shopped with other people before.

'You see, I never had the money to go shopping with my mates when they hit the shops on a Saturday afternoon,' she explained to Tatiana. 'And once I started work there was too much else to do. I used to rush out and buy my clothes in the lunch hour. You're right. This *is* fun.'

Tatiana guided her through a number of purchases. When they came to a discreet grey suit, though, Lisa dug her heels in. The velvet trim was timeless, but the waisted jacket was too old-fashioned, she complained.

'Look at me,' she said, turning this way and that in front of the mirror. 'It makes me look like Marilyn Monroe.'

'And you're complaining?' Tatiana shook her head reprovingly. 'If you've got it, flaunt it.'

Lisa flushed.

'You mustn't mind me.' Tatiana was amused, but slightly conscience-stricken. 'I say what I think.' She picked up a multi-coloured silk scarf and swirled it round Lisa's throat. 'Nicki and I are very alike in some ways,' she added casually.

And Lisa went positively scarlet. In fact she was so confused by this announcement that she allowed herself to buy the suit, a linen jacket and the scarf without a murmur of protest.

They took the purchases home. Lisa was quite happy to hang them up and take tea into the garden, but Tatiana was having none of it.

'Go and have a long smelly bath,' she said firmly. 'Then come up and give me a fashion show. I'll cook supper.'

'But—'

'Am I the expert or am I not?' demanded Tatiana.

'You are. You are. I'll do it,' said Lisa hastily.

She went.

And when she danced upstairs, dressed in the grey suit with a drift of golden silk georgette thrown round her long throat, the first person she saw was Nikolai. She stopped dead, all the lovely confidence collapsing.

'*Oh*. I'm sorry,' she said in disarray. 'I didn't know. I thought Tatiana was alone. I'll come back.'

But Nikolai, who had come to his feet with a start when she came in, said softly, 'Don't go.'

He was stunned. He had seen her sleepy and unwashed. He had seen her alert and firing on all cylinders at work. He had seen her hostile, and mischievous, and even vulnerable. He had never seen her like this.

The smooth lines of the suit gave her height, and an unexpected air of model-girl serenity. The drift of silk was like molten glass, reflected and reflecting the exquisite tints of ivory skin, gold hair, unexpected amber flecks in the green eyes.

'You look beautiful,' he said, astonished.

Lisa looked away. Her heart was fluttering peculiarly.

'You mean I look halfway respectable for once,' she said, too loudly. 'Tatiana—'

'—is on the telephone. When did this metamorphosis take place?'

'About three o'clock this afternoon.' Lisa's heartbeat was returning to normal. 'On Tatiana's advice.' She turned away. 'I'll come back when she's free.'

'You mean when I'm not here,' he interpreted. He took a step forward. 'Don't go because of me. I'm on my way out to dinner. I only stopped by for a minute.'

He didn't say that it would not have occurred to him if Tatiana had not called and asked him round specifically. He didn't know what game Tatiana was playing. But it was clear that it was not with Lisa's connivance.

'No,' she said firmly. 'Tell Tatiana I was here.'

She left by the French doors through which she had entered. Nikolai went to the window and watched her go down the spiral stairs.

Why had he not noticed before how gracefully she moved? In the evening sun her hair gleamed like gold. He felt that jerk of awareness again. It was becoming familiar.

When Tatiana came back into the room he said, 'You and I have to have a talk…'

Lisa's new appearance was greeted with a cheer by her disrespectful staff. But they could not make her blush.

'Grow up,' she told them, grinning, and concentrated all her attention on the screens.

It was not until the end of the day that Sam Voss appeared at her elbow.

'About time,' he said, fingering the sleeve of her tawny silk shirt. 'I hope you've got something long and frilly to go with it.'

Lisa removed her arm pointedly. 'Why?'

'Because you've got to take the Haraldsens to Glyndebourne on Friday.'

Lisa's heart sank. She got on all right with Leif

Haraldsen, who was a major portfolio investor, and she had met his wife a couple of times. But she had only hosted something for the bank once before, and that had been a relatively simple dinner.

'Why me?'

Sam wasn't pleased either. 'No idea. Special instruction from the Management Committee.'

'But I hate opera. And Glyndebourne is opera with knobs on, isn't it?' said Lisa.

She had heard stories of unbelievable glamour—and unbelievable pitfalls for the unwary party who had not been before.

Sam shrugged. 'I wouldn't know. I haven't been.' In the act of turning away he had another thought. He smiled and added maliciously, 'Oh, and you'll need an escort who owns a dinner jacket. What odds will the boys put on that, do you think?'

'The same as on any other project I run,' Lisa said calmly. 'They just look at my track record.'

Her eyes locked with Sam's. His were the first to fall.

Lisa was not as calm as she appeared, of course. She took the problem straight to Tatiana that night. She went up armed with a notebook and pen and sat at the dining table taking businesslike notes.

'OK. A dress. Does it have to be long?'

'Not if it's a Chanel original,' pronounced Tatiana. 'Glyndebourne's dressy but discreet. All the women will be trying to look as if they're upper-crust, and lots of them will be.'

Lisa put her pen down, a look of dismay on her face.

'It sounds like a minefield.'

'And I'm a style mine-detector,' said Tatiana with superb assurance. 'Trust me.'

'I do. But this happens on Friday. I haven't got time to go looking for a pair of tights, let alone Cinderella's gown for the ball,' said poor Lisa.

'Then let me do the looking. I know your size now. And I know more shops than you can imagine.'

That terrified Lisa even more. 'I'm still on a budget,' she warned Tatiana.

'Of course. Of course. Now, what about an escort?'

Lisa gave a choke of laughter, and couldn't stop.

'You don't have to find me one of those,' she said, when she had her breath back. 'Rob can hire a dinner jacket and come along.'

Tatiana looked dissatisfied. 'It's better to go with someone who's been before—knows the ropes, that sort of thing. And are you taking a picnic?'

Lisa abruptly lost all desire to laugh. 'Picnic?'

'See what I mean? You need an expert,' said Tatiana. 'Leave it to me.'

And Lisa did.

It was just as well that Tatiana did, indeed, know what she was doing. All that the Management Committee's superior secretary provided for Lisa was four tickets and a photocopy of a road map to Brighton.

'Sir Philip usually gets a picnic from Top Food,' she announced. 'When he found he couldn't go after all he told me to cancel it. Of course we'll reimburse you for anything you spend. Just bring in the receipts.'

'Great,' said Lisa, who had just written a hefty cheque to Mr Feldstein. 'Oh, well, I can put it on my credit card and sort it out later, I suppose.'

Tatiana took charge of that too. 'You'll have to call your guests and find out if they're allergic to anything. Then leave it to me.'

'I can't ask that of you,' protested Lisa. She was horrified at how much work seemed to be involved.

'I shall enjoy it.' She ticked it off on her fingers. 'There will be the picnic basket: food, champagne and nibbles for before the performance. Maybe another wine for dinner. A picnic table, folding chairs, tablecloth, candles…'

'Stop, stop,' cried Lisa in horror. 'It sounds like a military campaign.'

Tatiana took no notice of this feeble reaction.

'And find out whether they want to go down to Glyndebourne under their own steam or not. If they do, you'll need to send them their tickets so that they can get into the car park. If they don't, you'll have to organise transport from London,' said the irrepressible Tatiana. 'I'd think the bank would expect you to have a chauffeur-driven limousine.'

Lisa moaned.

But Tatiana was right. And without her enthusiastic support the whole project would have been a disaster. Especially when, out of the blue, Rob was sent to Copenhagen on Wednesday night.

'Sam did it deliberately,' raged Lisa. 'He *wants* me to mess up.'

'Very probably.' Tatiana was unmoved. 'Turn it to your advantage. I always thought you should take an escort who knew the ropes.'

'You?' said Lisa hopefully. 'I don't see why it has to be a man. We're listening to opera, not reproducing the species.'

Tatiana shook her head. 'Believe me, you'll be more comfortable with a man. And I know just the chap.'

Lisa gave up. Tatiana's advice had been a lifeline, after all.

'Oh, all right. Who—?' And then she realised. *'No!'*

'Nicki and Vladi started going to Glyndebourne when they were still at school,' Tatiana urged, hiding a smile. 'And Salzburg and Aix. And heaven knows where else as well. Their parents were mad about opera. If anyone can tell you what to do, it's Nicki.'

'But I've been trying to *stop* him telling me what to do ever since we met,' pointed out Lisa reasonably.

Tatiana was unsympathetic. 'Maybe it's time for you to listen to what he has to say.'

Lisa was torn. On the one hand she had promised herself that she would not see Nikolai Ivanov again. On the other she knew how much she was relying on Tatiana to help her clear the hurdle of Glyndebourne. In the end the latter won. But only just.

'All right,' she said morosely. 'But on the strict understanding that I'm only doing it for my career.'

Friday dawned clear and sunny.

'Good picnic weather,' said Tatiana, scenting the air professionally as Lisa shot past her on the doorstep.

Tatiana had been outraged that Lisa intended to go to work that morning.

'Glyndebourne is a whole-day project. You ought to spend the morning getting ready and relaxing,' she'd said.

But Lisa had laughed, and quoted the sliding Tokyo index. So Tatiana, under protest, had surrendered the dress and promised to have a car, with full picnic provided, collect Lisa at noon from Napier Kraus.

'But you must be changed and ready to go,' she'd warned.

'You sound like Cinderella's godmother,' Lisa had said, laughing. 'Do I turn back into a scarecrow at midnight?'

But now she gave Tatiana an uncharacteristic hug before she dashed off to work.

She was feeling less warm towards her four hours later. She stood in the ladies' cloakroom and inspected herself in the mirror with blank disbelief.

'Wow,' said Sam's secretary, pausing on her way out. Her astonishment was as great as Lisa's own. 'You look like a film star.'

Lisa shook her head. 'That's what comes of not trying things on,' she said grimly.

The secretary put her head on one side. 'Well, it fits.' She gave a wicked grin. 'Oh, boy, does it fit. If you let the dealing room see you in that they'll have a collective heart attack.'

'I know,' said Lisa.

She glared at her reflection. Tatiana had selected a slinky dress in some shot fabric, bronze in some lights, mineral-green in others. It had a long slim sleeve on one side and bared her shoulder on the other.

Lisa had worn less than this at clubs and parties all her life. But somehow she had never felt so naked. The very thought of Nikolai looking at her in this dress made her go hot and cold to her toes.

'I can't wear a bra with it,' she muttered.

The secretary prowled round her.

'I've got news for you, Lee. You can't wear knickers with it either,' she announced. 'Tights maximum.'

Lisa half turned, looking over her shoulder at her back view. The secretary was right. Lisa threw her mascara wand at the mirror.

When Nikolai swung the big car through the narrow City streets he was not in the best of moods. He'd wanted to see Lisa again, sure. He'd been *going* to see Lisa again. But when he decided and with her agreeing to it. Not when Tatiana had contrived it and they both felt manipulated. And certainly not with an audience of several hundred opera-goers and Mr and Mrs Leif Haraldsen.

He picked up the car phone and dialled Napier Kraus. 'Can you tell Ms Romaine I'll be there in five minutes? I probably won't be able to park, so if she could be waiting...'

Sam's secretary took the message. She went back to the cloakroom, where Lisa was still trying to convince herself that she looked the same as she always did.

'Your chauffeur wants you waiting on the steps. Better get going.'

Lisa gave her freshly washed hair a last fluff up. Made sure Tatiana's earrings were secure. Cast a harassed look at the glittering stranger in the mirror. Swallowed hard. And went.

CHAPTER SEVEN

NAPIER KRAUS had its offices in a steel and glass building
with a set of steps that would have been imposing on a
cathedral. Nikolai drew the rented Lexus to a halt at the foot
of the marble stairs and looked up with impatience. A long-
legged blonde was poised against the balustrade halfway
down, but otherwise the place was deserted.

The blonde was clearly a model. Somewhere there would
be a photographer or a film crew, though he couldn't see
them just at the moment. Maybe Lisa was waiting inside for
them to finish, he thought, trying to be reasonable. Well,
she would have to get a move on, before the car was towed
away for illegal parking.

He put on the hazard lights, left the engine running and
jumped out of the car. It was only as he ran lightly up the
steps that a thought occurred to him. An unwelcome
thought. He saw the blonde turn, start to come down the
steps towards him...

Lisa saw the car draw up with a lurch of alarm. There was
only one person in it and he was not wearing uniform. She
had subconsciously relied on the limousine driven by
Alfredo. But it looked as if Nikolai was going to drive her
himself.

The Haraldsens were going straight to Glyndebourne. So
that just left the two of them in the close confines of the
car. All the way there. And worse, all the way back, when
she would be tired and Nikolai would feel licensed to ask
whatever he wanted under the liberating cover of darkness.
She nearly turned on her heel and dived back into the
building.

But then he got out of the car and came up the steps. It was too late.

'You look—different,' he greeted her.

He did not seem pleased about it.

'Take it up with my style counsellor,' Lisa said flippantly. 'The dress was Tatiana's choice.'

'Tatiana?' He sounded outraged. 'But I told her—' He stopped abruptly.

Lisa didn't notice. She began to move carefully down the steps. The heels on the shoes Tatiana had selected were higher and slimmer than she had ever worn before. She was tempted to grab Nikolai's arm for balance. She resisted.

He seemed impatient. 'We'd better shift. We don't want your guests to get there before us.'

He ran back down the steps and held the car door. Lisa concentrated hard. There was a real risk of spearing the long skirt with one of her *poignard* heels, and she was not carrying a repair kit.

She thought, I bet the girls he normally takes out never move without a needle and thread and an insurance pack of safety pins. I can pretend all I like that I'm used to going to the ball, but what happens the moment something goes wrong? I will have no idea how to handle it.

'Thank you,' she said with constraint.

As she turned to do up her seat belt the split skirt gaped from thigh to ankle. She was, he saw, wearing black tights so sheer they looked as if they would dissolve if you just breathed on them. He had never imagined her in anything so sophisticated. He did not like it. And yet—

'You're welcome,' said Nikolai with equal constraint.

It took them nearly an hour to get out of London. Lisa conscientiously tried not to distract Nikolai by talking, though he weaved his way through the south London streets with an unconcerned expertise which suggested he had done it many times before. For some reason it made her heart sink.

Lisa knew Tatiana had been right when she'd said Lisa

needed an expert to escort her. The trouble was Lisa would rather have gone with anyone but Nikolai. He mistrusted her, and said so. He despised her, and made no secret of it. Up to now Lisa had been able to tell herself she didn't care, because she hadn't tried to pretend she was anything that she was not.

But now! Every single thing about her was pretence. From the sophisticated clothes to her role as official host, she was playing a part. And it was a part he would see right through. Because Nikolai Ivanov was the real thing.

So when she sat silent beside him, it was not entirely out of concern for his concentration.

She thought, He'll know I'm a phoney. Because I *am*.

Eventually they were out of the suburbs and the signposts were saying Brighton. Nikolai increased speed. He glanced at his passenger. She was still preoccupied—and not very happily, he thought.

Lisa was different today. It was not just the clothes, though they changed her almost beyond recognition. The sophisticated dress made her look taller, more poised than he would have imagined possible. But it was not the dress or the shoes or Tatiana's amethysts. It was her quietness.

This was not the woman who had glared at the unknown man on her doorstep, who had had no compunction in screaming at the top of her voice in the street to get rid of him, who argued and challenged and infuriated him at every step. This was a stranger.

It felt wrong. Nikolai was puzzled at how wrong it felt. They were not strangers now.

He said slowly, 'I feel as if I ought to be polite to you.'

Lisa winced. *Phoney* her mind screamed.

To disguise her unease, she said sharply, 'Why change the habit of a lifetime?'

Nikolai relaxed. *Welcome back*, he exulted. But silently.

'It isn't a lifetime. It only seems like it.'

'Then why don't you go back to France? Then you won't have to endure me any more.'

'Not until I've got what I came for.'

Lisa shrugged. 'Well, don't force yourself to be polite on my account. I'm not used to being buttered up. It just makes me uncomfortable.'

Nikolai glanced down at the gleaming gold hair. A faint scent of apple blossom seemed to rise as she shook her head. It was a fresh, innocent perfume, totally at odds with today's image.

Amused, he said, 'You are a complete chameleon. I can't think of one single thing that would make you uncomfortable.'

'But you don't know me very well,' said Lisa with desperate honesty.

He didn't notice. He gave that sexy laugh and said, 'I know you better than you think.'

The trouble was he *believed* it.

Oh, boy, am I in trouble, thought Lisa.

She said, gabbling, 'Look, I've never been to Glyndebourne before. I could make a real fool of myself.'

But even that didn't seem to warn him.

'Yes, Tatiana said,' he agreed calmly. 'Don't worry, there's a first time for everything.'

She looked up in sudden suspicion. But his expression was innocent and his eyes were on the road.

'So brief me,' she said, after the tiniest pause.

Nikolai bit back a smile.

'Well, the house is in the fold of three hills. It is very old and beautiful, and the garden is like the best sort of English cottage garden but on a grand scale. Originally the opera house was built in the old stables, I think. But these days there's a new auditorium with wonderful acoustics.'

Lisa shook her head. 'It's a crazy place for a theatre.'

'Quite. That's why the operas always start so early.'

Lisa had memorised the details. 'The ticket says half past six.'

'That's because it's Janáček, and relatively short. Mozart can start as early as five. They break everything into two.

Halfway through there's a supper interval of about an hour and a half. There are several restaurants where you can eat but traditionalists prefer a picnic in the gardens.'

Lisa sniffed. 'We'll have to eat fast,' she said, thinking of the list of provisions that Tatiana had insisted were necessary.

Nikolai laughed. 'When I first came we used to bring a bottle of champagne and a simple salad. Now everything is more elaborate—and very expensive.'

'I know *that*,' said Lisa. 'The bank buys tickets every year. But normally no one below the Management Committee gets to take the guests along.'

'I'm not surprised,' Nikolai said drily. 'I'm afraid it's become rather smart. Hence the dinner jackets and champagne.' He smiled suddenly. 'But it's worth it for the music. Six weeks' rehearsal and some of the best young singers in the world. That's as good as opera gets.'

Lisa shifted uncomfortably. She didn't say anything, but Nikolai picked up the message clearly enough.

'Don't like opera?'

'Well, I've only seen one,' Lisa admitted. 'It drove me crazy.'

He didn't laugh at her. 'Why?'

'They kept singing about stuff instead of getting on and doing it,' she said honestly. She sent him a defiant look. 'OK, I'm an oik. I can't get worked up about things that have nothing to do with real life.'

Still he didn't laugh at her. He just nodded, as if she had said something completely reasonable.

'You'll find this evening's opera is real life, all right. It's about a woman married to a weak man whose life is made hell by her mother-in-law.'

Lisa detected a put-down. 'I suppose you know it backwards,' she said resigned. 'Well, go on, then; tell me the story.'

'That's about it. Katya Kabanova is very gentle and well behaved. But her husband turns out to be an alcoholic who is completely under his mother's thumb. She hates Katya, who falls in love with another man, gets caught in a thunderstorm, decides it's a punishment and drowns herself in the Volga.'

'Cheerful.'

'Well, Katya doesn't have your resolution,' Nikolai said, his lips twitching. 'I can't see you letting the mother-in-law bully the life out of you.'

Lisa looked at him suspiciously. 'You buttering me up again, Boris?'

Nikolai looked genuinely taken aback. Then his eyes began to dance.

'Not at all. She abandons herself to love, Katya. Even believing that it will end in death. I don't see you doing that either.'

'Love!' said Lisa scornfully. 'The only thing it ends in is a great big pie in the face.'

Nikolai's shoulders shook. 'I'm sure you're right.' He negotiated a roundabout, then said airily, 'Oh, by the way, you should be prepared. The man she's in love with—'

'Well?' said Lisa.

'He's called Boris.'

And his laughter bubbled over.

There was a moment's silence. Lisa stared at him in disbelief. Then her shoulders, too, began to shake.

'I don't *believe* it!'

'True, I'm afraid.'

'That will teach me,' said Lisa ruefully. 'I won't call you Boris again.' A thought occurred to her. 'I could have called you that in front of the Haraldsens. Then the opera might have made them think there was something more than business between us.' She began to laugh again, but her laughter was hollow. 'Oh God, I'll be lucky if I get through this without dropping a king-size clanger.'

But all went like clockwork. Entirely because of Nikolai's smooth stage management.

They reached the Elizabethan house mid-afternoon.

Nikolai tucked the picnic basket under his arm and walked
her briskly into the grounds. They went through an orchard,
where they were warned not to step on the wild orchids and,
while Lisa was still reeling from this extraordinary instruction, he steered her past bowers of early roses and a walled
garden to a long, shimmering lake.

'It's like one of those paintings,' Lisa said. Simple delight
had made her forget how uneducated she was in comparison
with Nikolai. 'Beautiful ladies in pointy hats picking golden
apples in Paradise.'

One eyebrow flicked up in surprise. 'Well, a hat wouldn't
go down well with the people behind you in the theatre,'
he said drily. 'And only a vandal would pick anything. But
I get your drift.'

He gave her a smile so sweet that Lisa blinked. Then,
awkwardly, smiled back. Maybe he wasn't going to put her
down after all.

'Here,' he said, depositing the basket under a willow.
'Wait for your guests and I'll get the rest.'

So, by the time the Haraldsens wandered up, the picnic
table was set, the champagne open and Lisa was stretched
out in her canvas chair gazing dreamily up through the willow's golden-green branches. She gave the Haraldsens a
wide, lazy smile.

'Isn't this perfect?'

Bees hummed.

'It surely is,' agreed Leif Haraldsen, helping his wife to
champagne and one of Tatiana's cheese straws. 'It was real
good of you to step in like this, Lisa.'

Quite suddenly the occasion stopped being a burden.

It still had its sticky moments, of course. Strolling beside
the lake while Monika Haraldsen probed delicately into her
relationship with Nikolai Ivanov was one. Not having provided one of the book sized programmes for her guests was
another.

Nikolai dealt with that. He disappeared and returned with
four before she had finished apologising.

But the worst, by far, was at the end of the supper interval. The food had been delicious, the wine perfect. The twilight had fallen to a cool delight. All around them there was muted laughter. Leif was taking a photograph of the house. Monika and Nikolai were chatting about the opera.

And suddenly Lisa felt someone looking at her. Not looking, staring. She looked up. Far away, across the green lawn, a man was standing on the edge of a knot of people, his eyes fixed on her. She frowned. He was too far away to recognise—all the men looked vaguely alike in their uniform of dinner jackets—but there was something familiar about him all the same.

When he saw her looking he turned to his party, very deliberately put down the glass he was holding, and came over. As he made his way round picnickers and people strolling to savour the scents of evening, Lisa saw who it was. Her skin seemed to freeze on her bones.

'Lee! I thought it was you.'

Nikolai interrupted his conversation with Monika and stood up courteously.

'Hello, Terry,' said Lisa through frozen lips.

'Hi, doll. Long time no see.'

He bent and kissed her without hesitation. She turned her head away, so that the kiss landed somewhere in the area of her ear. She too stood up.

'May I introduce Terry Long? He was with Napier Kraus for a while. Terry, Mrs Haraldsen, Count Ivanov.'

And I even introduced them the right way round, thought Lisa with mild hysteria. Tatiana would have been proud of me.

It was a shame that she didn't have the energy to feel pleased with herself for that minor special achievement. But Lisa was beyond it. She was feeling as if she had walked into a wall.

Terry didn't help. He didn't actually say anything crude, but his amused disbelief when she introduced Nikolai said it all. And he put his arm round her waist as if he had the right to.

Lisa moved away. But not before Nikolai had registered the movement. His reaction was quite unreadable, but she still hated him seeing Terry's gesture of ritual possession.

'Lee and I haven't seen each other in a long time,' Terry told the others expansively. He looked her up and down, his eyes lingering on her bared shoulder. 'You've come a long way, doll.'

Lisa held herself together with fierce concentration. Her flesh shrank from his knowledgeable eyes. How could I ever have trusted this creep? she thought. She was frozen with humiliation. She couldn't think of a thing to say.

Again, it was Nikolai who saved the situation. He offered Terry a drink, changed the subject, and kept it changed until someone came to announce the three-minute warning. In the flurry of packing up the basket and folding the chairs Lisa somehow managed to blank Terry out of her consciousness.

It didn't last, of course. As soon as they were settled in the darkened auditorium she was alone with her emotions. The music was wild and dark. Years of dammed-up misery and shame surged through her in response. As poor, guilt-ridden Katya drove herself to death, Lisa found tears welling uncontrollably.

Her head was so thick with them that she could hardly breathe. A breath emerged as a snuffle. She cringed with embarrassment.

A hand nudged hers. Looking down, she saw Nikolai pushing a white handkerchief under her fingers. She swallowed and took it. She couldn't look at him.

Afterwards it was not mentioned.

'Let's have a coffee,' he said. 'They serve it at the bar, and otherwise we'll just have to sit for ages in the queue to get out of the car park.'

He managed it all, chatting with the Haraldsens so cheerfully that they didn't even notice that Lisa was suddenly withdrawn. She made enough of an effort to say a proper goodbye when they left, and to go with him to collect the remains of the picnic.

'It's so dark,' she said, as they plunged out of the light of the auditorium complex into the trees.

Nikolai produced a pencil torch from his pocket. 'Sorted.'

'Very efficient.' It was easier to sound normal under cover of darkness.

'Never underestimate an explorer,' he said solemnly.

As if to prove his point he gathered up the basket and the picnic furniture, disposing them about his body as if he were a human mule. Lisa found that all she was carrying was a wine cooler and the torch.

'You really have done this before, haven't you?' she said, trying to sound impressed.

How long can I keep this up? she thought wretchedly.

'Never quite like this.' Was it her imagination or did he sound unwontedly serious?

They went back through the orchard, Lisa leading with the torch. She walked through the unclipped grasses carefully. But not carefully enough. Eventually she turned her slim heel. The beam swung wildly. She staggered.

And Nikolai caught her to his side.

His arm was hot under the black cloth of his jacket. She could feel his blood racing. If she let her head fall back it would fall against his shoulder, and if she looked up... Lisa's imagination went into free association. Her breath stopped in her throat at the images it was coming up with.

'H-how did you do that?' she said distractedly. 'You were carrying so much. What have you done with it?'

Nikolai sounded oddly shaken. 'Quick reflexes. I threw the chairs away.'

'Oh.'

She was breathing again, but too fast. All around them the sounds of a summer night rippled and eddied. Her imagination carried on motoring.

Lisa thought, I'm waiting for him to kiss me! I don't

believe this! He's weighed down like a porter and I expect him to kiss me?

She pulled herself together. 'I hope you didn't crush any of the orchids.' It was a poor attempt at lightness but it was all she could manage.

She removed herself from his sustaining arm. Then she took off her shoes, hung them from one hand and picked up the chairs. Nikolai did not protest. She had a feeling he was as shaken by his reflex reaction as she was.

They went back to the car in silence.

The silence continued until they were on the outskirts of London. It had been raining, and sodium lights were reflected back from puddles in the road. The dark cityscape was tinged with a strange other-worldliness.

'It looks as if we're driving through a wormhole,' said Lisa involuntarily.

Nikolai sent her a quick look.

'You're a science fiction addict, right?'

She was immediately on the defensive. 'I suppose you think that's very silly.'

'Why should I think any such thing?'

'Well—you're a real scientist, aren't you?'

'And all scientific theories are fiction until someone comes up with the evidence,' Nikolai said calmly. 'I can't afford to despise anyone for liking science fiction, believe me. They're the people who sponsor expeditions.'

'Do you need sponsors, then? I thought—'

'You thought I was very rich,' Nikolai said with an edge to his voice. 'You thought I gathered up a few chums and went hunting in the jungle like some Victorian dilettante.'

'No,' said Lisa, taken aback by his vehemence.

'My research is not a hobby. I earn my living from it. Oh, on paper the family is rich, sure. On paper we're no doubt millionaires. That's the family, mind. Not me.'

'I didn't mean—'

He took no notice of her small protest. 'But most of the wealth is in land and houses and paintings and furniture. If

don't want to eat the furniture, I need to keep on working.
And that means fieldwork and writing papers and lecturing.'
He sounded furious. 'Not something to be sneered at, even
by someone who thinks wealth is the most important thing
in the world.'

Lisa raised her voice. 'OK. OK. I'm sorry I leaped to
conclusions. I didn't mean to sneer at your work, all right?'
After a moment she added in a mutter, 'And I don't think
wealth is the most important thing in the world.'

They were approaching traffic lights. They were the only
car in the silent street. He narrowed his eyes at the lights
and said quietly, 'Then how come you do the work you
do?'

Lisa's chin came up. She almost didn't answer him. But
there was something about the darkness of the car, the emp-
tiness of the streets, the silence, that made intimacy somehow inescapable.

After a moment she said with difficulty, 'I told you
once—people on the edge of survival talk a lot about
money.'

There was a complicated silence. Then Nikolai said, 'On
the edge of survival? You?'

'Oh, I'm a fat cat now,' Lisa said drily. 'It was different
when I was growing up.'

He waited. But she didn't say any more.

They were crossing Albert Bridge. The swathes of its sus-
pension cables were picked out with lights like drops of
pearls. It looked like a fairy bridge over the black ribbon of
the river.

'So what was it like when you were growing up?' he
prompted at last.

Maybe because she was so tired, Lisa had the illusion
that they were travelling in a capsule, out of time and space.
It felt as if it didn't matter what she told him. The journey
would go on for ever and she would never have to face
tomorrow.

So she told him what she had never told anyone, not even Terry.

'When I was growing up there was nothing,' she said dreamily. 'No money. No settled home. Just a series of rented rooms wherever Mother could find them. No friends, because we kept moving on. Not much education for the same reason. Maybe that was why—' She stopped abruptly.

Nikolai was very still. 'Why...?' he prompted at last.

Lisa gave a long sigh. 'Why Kit has such a tough time with life.'

'Who is Kit?' His voice was very soft.

As if she were a wild animal he didn't want to alarm, Lisa thought. She smiled. In the warm cocoon of the car, as the silent street slid past the window, she had almost forgotten what it was like to be alarmed.

'Kit is my younger sister. She was diagnosed anorexic when she was thirteen. She's twenty now. They say she's over the worst of it. We keep hoping.'

Nikolai nodded, as if he knew something about the condition. 'She slips back?'

'Every time she gets an emotional knock. Never as bad as the first time.' Lisa sighed, then said with that strange, disembodied honesty, 'In fact, sometimes I wonder if my mother is imagining it. But then Kit runs away from something she's afraid of and it all seems to start again.'

'I have a friend who works with recovering anorexics. It can be tough on the families.' He sent her a quick look. 'How do your other family members react to her behaviour?'

'I told you—that *is* the family. Kit, me and Mum.'

Nikolai was gentle. 'Your father is dead?'

Lisa shrugged. 'Shouldn't think so. He pushed off when I was a baby. We survived.'

He said blankly, 'But—support? Money, if nothing else? Haven't you tried to contact him?'

'You think a man should have come along and sorted us out.' Lisa was too amused to be offended. 'Fat chance.' She

istened to what she had said and then shook her head, dissatisfied. 'Don't get me wrong. I wouldn't want a man sort-
ng out my life for me. Maybe my mother would have liked
some input when we were kids. But these days it's not necessary. I can support the family.'

He was stunned.

Just to make sure he understood, she added, 'I'm independent, and I like it that way.'

She sent him a little challenging look from under her
lashes. He was frowning.

'Do you?' he said heavily.

She was flippant. 'The only way for a modern girl to live.
Means you're not answerable to anyone.'

They were driving north, through smarter and smarter
streets.

'Trees and gardens,' she said suddenly. 'You can always
tell where the rich live. Wide streets, plenty of trees, and
the houses have gardens.'

His voice was harsh. 'Is that why you moved in on
Tatiana? So you could live the rich life, with a garden?'

Lisa went very still.

'I'm sorry.' He sounded strained. 'I shouldn't have said
that. It wasn't part of today's bargain, was it?'

'Today's bargain?'

They were going up Notting Hill. In the light from the
streetlamps Lisa could see a muscle working in his jaw. He
swung the car off the main street as if it were a personal
enemy.

'The standard sexual deal. You look beautiful. I take care
of you.' Nikolai's tone was husky.

Lisa said, 'It wasn't like that…'

'And when it's over we both say a graceful thank you
and goodnight.'

He parked the car and killed the headlights. At once the
interior of the car was very dark. He seemed amazingly
close. The illusion of the capsule disappeared. He was too
close, too warm, his breathing too loud.

Lisa moistened suddenly dry lips. 'G-goodnight.'

It sounded horrifyingly tremulous, she thought in disgust. And after she had been claiming her independence so proudly. He would have every right to think that she didn't know her own mind. Or, worse, that she had been putting it on for some devious feminine reason.

He turned and looked at her. 'Or maybe we don't.'

The silence was charged. Lisa couldn't think of a thing to say.

The quiet streets were darker here. She couldn't make a guess at his expression. She could barely make out his outline.

And then he moved, and, whether by accident or design, his hand brushed against her bare arm.

Lisa gave a strangled choke. It was the same uncontrollable sound that had betrayed her in the auditorium. She felt Nikolai relax in the darkness.

'We're here,' he said softly.

As if she were in a dream, Lisa let him help her out of the car, and, with his arm round her, lead her into the block of flats where he was staying. The night air was cool where her skin was exposed. She didn't feel it. She only felt the heat of his hand in the small of her back, burning through the material like a brand.

She thought, *This has been waiting for us since the day we met.*

He didn't say anything, not even when they went inside and he put on the low lamps. The room was too full of old furniture, and it seemed as if books and papers covered every surface. Beyond the lamps Lisa saw walls covered with pictures. She'd not noticed so much detail on her first visit to his flat. Her heart contracted with despair. More pictures. More antiques. More *wealth*.

'We are so different,' she said.

'I'm a man. You're a woman. That's usually considered a good start.'

Lisa didn't smile. She knew there had been a time when

she'd considered men a joke, but at this moment she couldn't even remember what it had felt like. She was shaking.

She didn't want him to sense it. She moved away from him and stared blindly at the contents of a break front bookcase.

'This is not the sort of thing I normally do.'

'What sort of thing?' There was a smile in his voice.

Lisa was beyond smiling. She fixed her eyes on a leatherbound volume of Browning's poems.

'Sex with a stranger,' she said bitterly.

He watched her for a moment, silent.

'Hardly a stranger.'

'You don't listen, do you? I told you today. You don't know me very well. In fact you don't know me at all.'

Nikolai didn't answer. Or not with words.

He came up behind her. She could see his shadow in the glass of the bookcase. He bent his head and Lisa tensed. But he didn't kiss her. Instead he moved his cheek, as if he were caressing the air above her bare shoulder. Or smelling her skin. Lisa's body clenched in pure lust.

'Do you want to go home?'

This was her chance. This was where she said yes, it was a mistake, she had changed her mind. This was where she *escaped*.

'No,' said Lisa.

With his hands on her, Lisa could no longer disguise from him how deeply she was trembling. She braced herself for mockery. Once again he was proving his point. Only far, far more devastatingly than he had in the club.

But he did not mock. Instead he set his mouth against the side of her throat. No teasing the air this time; it was a real kiss. Lisa felt his tongue against her skin and gave a shivery moan. She flung herself round in his arms, quickly, *hungrily*.

Through the dress, his hands were like fire on her hips. He clamped her to him so she felt the force of his arousal. And the hot response of her own. She made a small, needy sound that startled her. But not Nikolai. Utterly in control, he bent his head and explored the tender places at the base of her throat, her earlobes, her eyelids. It was a deliberate torment. Lisa's flesh ached.

She could bear no more. She caught his head and held it for her kiss, as clumsy as if she were a teenager on her first date. And then he gave her the mastery she hadn't known she wanted. His tongue probed her mouth ruthlessly.

She couldn't think. She couldn't breathe. She just pressed herself to him blindly.

He raised his head and said huskily, 'We'll be more comfortable in the bedroom.'

In a fevered dream Lisa felt herself picked up and put on the bed. He was unzipping the sophisticated dress in a practised movement.

She thought, *He has done this before.* It chilled her for a moment. But then he plucked the glittering stuff over her head and threw it. Lisa gasped. She glimpsed it behind his shoulders, a bolt of phosphorescence against the dark.

Then his mouth found her breast and her eyes lost focus altogether. Her nipples rose, wanton. Every muscle in her body tautened in anticipation. She could only cling to him, trembling with the helplessness of her need.

Nikolai made a low sound in his throat. Of pleasure? Triumph? Lisa did not know. Both, perhaps? Lust? No doubt at all about that. And it was mutual.

He raised his head and looked down at her body. Her breasts were hot and swollen. He drew a startled breath. Then suddenly he was pushing her back among the pillows, his hands urgent on her skin. He was no longer in such exquisite control.

She was wearing nothing but those sheer tights now. Nikolai began to roll them voluptuously over her hip bones. His mouth followed the same path. His hands were agonisingly slow but his mouth was passionate. Lisa sobbed aloud.

And then she was naked. The pre-dawn air made her

breasts start. But although she was shivering helplessly, it was not with cold. Nikolai kissed her stomach, the jut of her hips, her quivering thighs. His breathing was ragged.

The ache between her thighs was like a scream. She had no will left for anything except the one, the only goal. And Nikolai knew it. He set his mouth to the sweet pulsing centre of her and Lisa cried out in raw need. She didn't recognise her voice. It sounded like a little girl's. And as old as time.

Nikolai paused. He raised his head. In the near dark, he and Lisa stared at each other.

Tiny tremors took her, like the precursor of an earthquake. She did her best to ignore them. Oh, yes, she had been right. The attention he bent on her was concentrated, terrifying. And utterly seductive.

He said harshly, 'This is not sex with a stranger.'

Lisa was beyond pretence, beyond shame. She flung up her chin. 'Then take your clothes off.'

It was a challenge. They both knew it. For a moment they glared into each other's eyes like enemies.

'Then help me,' said Nikolai, in a fierce challenge of his own.

She thrust herself up from the pillows, reaching. A jacket flew through the shadows and he began to tear at his shirt. Lisa plucked at the bow tie, her fingers frantic with the unfamiliar thing, her blood roaring.

'Please,' she said under her breath. 'Please, please, *please*.'

She didn't know if she was talking to herself or him or the damned tie. Nikolai had no doubt. He detached her fingers, flicked the tie free and cast it away. Lisa fell back as he rid himself of the rest of his clothes.

He bent over her, his eyes relentless in the grey dawn. 'A stranger?'

She was reverberating like a plucked string, hardly daring to breathe.

'Nikolai—' It was half-plea, half-groan.

'The man who came over to us this evening,' he said at last roughly. 'Was he the one who didn't turn up? At the awards, I mean.'

'What?' For a moment Lisa didn't know what he was talking about. When she realised, she couldn't believe it. It was so ridiculous she could have laughed. Or she could if she hadn't been so close to the edge of distraction.

'Was he?' His tone demanded an answer.

Lisa made a ragged sound of protest. 'No.'

'Then who was it? That boy said you were angry because some man wasn't there. *Who?*' He sounded as if he was on the rack.

Lisa's body was arching, way beyond her control.

'Sam,' she gasped.

He thrust a powerful thigh between hers, kissing her forcefully. Lisa's eyes fluttered shut uncontrollably. She reached for him. But he still held off from the ultimate invasion.

'Who is this Sam? Sam Voss, from work?'

'What?' Lisa's head tossed on the pillow. 'Why? Oh, Nikolai—'

But he was implacable. 'Who is he?'

'Yes, my boss.' Her breathing was a wild sob. 'Why—?'

'I'm going to make you forget him,' said Nikolai.

He tugged her limbs around him. She felt the shock of masculine muscles contracting, the absolute potency of his knowledge of her body, and then—at last—his hardness inside her. Lisa strained to meet him, driving, driven, her whole body slamming in shockingly powerful demand.

He didn't ask her what she wanted. Or not in words. He let her body tell him. And it did.

'You—want—me,' he said.

And took her over the edge.

CHAPTER EIGHT

AFTERWARDS Lisa lay in his arms, utterly content. The darkened room was lit only by fuzzy reflected light from the street. In the Gothic shadows she could feel Nikolai watching her. She liked him watching her.

His hand stroked her shoulder rhythmically, almost absently. It was a gesture of total possession. To her private astonishment, Lisa gloried in it. She rubbed her face against his chest, savouring the roughness of hair under her cheek, the unique smell of him.

'Tell me now that I don't know anything about you,' he invited. There was a smile in his voice.

She kissed his chest drowsily. 'Oh you do. You do.'

'Are you still quite sure you don't need a man to sort out your life?' he teased.

But Lisa was hovering on the edge of sleep.

'Whatever you say,' she murmured.

'Excellent.'

Nikolai paused, waiting for an indignant rebuttal. But Lisa was asleep.

In the darkness, his smile died. He gathered her closer; so close, indeed, that she turned, murmuring a small protest in her sleep. He relaxed his grip fractionally and she subsided against him with a sigh of satisfaction.

'Lisa,' he said. Then, louder, as if he were testing it out, 'Lisa, darling.'

She murmured indecipherably. Nikolai waited, but she didn't make another sound. He shifted her, very gently, and drew the covers up over her naked shoulders. He kissed her hair.

And then he, too, slept.

* * *

In the cold light of day, of course, everything changed.

Lisa woke up in a rush, bounced out of a dream in which she was walking down an endless staircase in wobbly heels towards a man who kept hiding his face from her. She sat bolt upright, exclaiming *'No!'* before she even realised that it had been a dream.

Nikolai appeared in the bedroom door. He was wearing horribly sexy black jeans and nothing else. Even his feet were bare. Lisa went scarlet.

He, however, was completely unembarrassed. 'Sorry, missed that,' he said cheerfully.

Which reminded her all too effectively of what she had thought last night: *He has done this before.* Many times, if she was any judge.

She hauled the sheets up to her chin, and said with as much dignity as she could manage, 'I was dreaming.'

He grinned. 'Who needs to dream?'

Lisa met his eyes. Suddenly all the things they had done to each other last night were there in the room with them, like music. Her pulses began to beat in slow, thunderous tempo.

Nikolai discarded his jeans. Lisa's lashes fell to her suddenly hot cheeks.

His hands knew her now. He hauled her up against his body, knowing exactly how the sweet friction of skin on skin would drive her wild. Lisa's breath quickened and her head fell back.

His mouth tugged and sucked at her breast until she was mindless. She kicked the sheets away, pulling him back onto the bed with her. Nikolai responded by swirling her up out of the ruin of the sheets and turning her over.

'Not fair,' said Lisa, drumming her fists on the pillow. She was half laughing, half seriously off balance. 'Let me touch you.'

'In a minute.' His voice was husky.

Nikolai caught her wrists in one hand and held her down.

His lips travelled softly along the line of her ribs, her spine. Lisa shivered in an agony of exquisite anticipation.

'I always knew I liked butterflies,' he murmured.

Lisa felt his lips against the tattoo on her shoulderblade. It became difficult to breathe.

'I promised myself this weeks ago.' His voice was ragged.

Lisa's body was juddering. He can't make me feel like this with just a kiss, she thought. He *can't*.

But he did.

She buried her face in the pillow and came to a moaning climax.

'Not fair,' he said in her ear.

And turned her over again. He scanned her flushed face as if every tiny ripple of sensation was a personal triumph.

Lisa's head whirled. She felt proud and yet humble, shy and yet shameless. Utterly in his power and yet, when she folded herself round him and let her confident hands move, as powerful as a goddess.

He shuddered, groaning as she wrapped her legs round him like a vice.

'Not—yet—' His voice was almost unrecognisable. But he was still master of her responses.

Lisa writhed as he used hands and mouth to bring her again and again to the point of dissolution.

'What are you doing to me?' she gasped.

His eyes burned into hers. They were on the floor by now, in a mess of sheets, blankets and pillows.

'What are you doing to me?' he flung back at her.

Even his immaculate control seemed to be deserting him now. He was breathless and his voice shook.

For a moment he held her beneath him, one hand running through her damp hair, his eyes blazing like the heart of a furnace. Lisa's lips parted.

'Oh, God, you only have to look at me.' It was only a whisper, but it sounded as if it was torn out of him.

Lisa couldn't endure the waiting any longer. Shaking, she

reached for him and guided him inside her. His face tensed until she could see the bones under the tautened skin. A muscle throbbed in his cheek.

For a moment his expression was wild. And then his eyes shut and he abandoned himself to a passion that took her, violently, on the rollercoaster with him.

They both cried out. Only in her case it felt like weeping.

Later—much later—he stirred and said lazily, 'What do you normally do on Saturdays?'

Lisa was beyond embarrassment. She was not, however, beyond cold. She sat up and looked for something to put round her.

'Washing,' she said literally. Continuing, 'Haven't you got anything I can wear?'

He propped himself up against the wall and surveyed her. He looked inordinately pleased with himself.

'What's wrong with your own clothes? I rather fancy you in a Krizia Karlton original.'

'You fancy me in anything,' said Lisa drily.

His eyes were golden, and so warm she hardly recognised him.

'Or nothing,' he reminded her.

Lisa choked. 'How could I forget?'

'Not good for my morale,' he agreed. He stood up, magnificently naked, and rootled behind a dressing stool. 'There you are,' he said retrieving a glittering piece of cloth with triumph.

He gave it to her.

'Thank you,' said Lisa without enthusiasm. She held it up between finger and thumb. It looked even more revealing than she remembered. 'How am I going to walk home through the Saturday shoppers in this?'

'You'll just have to stay here till dark.'

'A gentleman would lend me something to wear.'

'Well, you're welcome to anything that fits,' he offered wickedly. 'There are some tasteful tablecloths in the bathroom airing cupboard. Try one of them.'

'I might,' she said with dignity. '*After* my bath.'

'I'll put the coffee on.'

Lisa filled the bath with steaming water, added some drops of a luxurious essence of white lilac that she found on the shelf, and sank back luxuriously. She had never felt so utterly physically content in her life.

Nikolai, she thought, stirring the water dreamily, was a wonderful lover. He seemed to pour the whole of himself into it, as if he could make time stand still by the very intensity of his feelings. It must be his passionate Russian blood, she decided.

Of course, he hadn't actually said he loved her. But then who needed him to, when he touched her the way he did? His body said it for him. Besides, as she had told Alec, she had learned long ago not to trust declarations of love.

Who am I kidding? I want him to say he loves me. I want it more than anything in the world.

'Top marks for consistency, Lisa,' she muttered.

But somehow the thought spoiled her sybaritic enjoyment. She got out of the bath.

It was only when she came to put the dress on that she saw the label. 'K2' it said in discreet embroidered script. Lisa grinned, remembering how easily Nikolai had identified the designer. Krizia Karlton was presumably 'K2'.

Altogether too practised, she thought, and went looking for him to tease him on his knowledge of female designer wear.

And as she went past the books, the gleaming antiques, the picture-hung walls, she began to think. She had never heard of Krizia Karlton. And the label, though it was a clue, was not specific. So how *did* Nikolai know who had designed her dress?

By the time she reached the kitchen, her body was taut with suspicion. Even so, if he had denied it, or given a halfway plausible excuse, she would have accepted it. She so *wanted* to accept it. But he did not.

He shrugged, unconcerned. 'OK. It's a fair cop.'

'A fair cop?' Lisa didn't understand.

'I wanted you to have something pretty to wear. It was such a waste, Tatiana getting you to buy all that stuff from thrift shops, no matter how up market they were. I told her to get you a real dress.'

'You—bought—my—dress?'

'So what? You liked it, didn't you?' He gave her a wicked grin. 'I certainly did.'

It was Terry Long, all over again. *You're fun trash, Lisa Romaine.* Her eyes hurt.

'Were you afraid of what I would wear to Glyndebourne? Didn't you want to risk me disgracing you? After all, we might have seen some of your friends there, mightn't we?'

He blinked at her savage tone.

'Hey, I wanted to give you a present, that was all.'

'No, it wasn't.' Her voice was so quiet it was almost inaudible. 'If you'd wanted to give me a present, you would have given it to me. Not conspired with Tatiana so that I thought I'd bought it myself—' She broke off and swallowed several times. 'Tell me the truth, Nikolai.'

He sighed impatiently. 'All right. The truth is that I knew you wouldn't take it from me. And I was—'

'Planning,' supplied Lisa. She thought her heart would break.

'What?'

'That's what this is about, isn't it? The Ivanov family plan to protect their own.'

Nikolai began to be seriously alarmed. 'Don't be ridiculous. I wouldn't have gone to bed with you or any woman to protect Tatiana.'

'No,' Lisa agreed. She sounded, even to herself, as remote as the moon. But at least she sounded in control again, thank God. 'No, I imagine taking me to bed was a bonus.'

'That's crazy.'

Lisa was very cold. She clutched her arms round herself protectively. When her hand touched her own bared shoul-

ler she shuddered in shocked recollection. Her chin came
ιp.

'My mother always told me that if you let a man buy you
clothes, he'd expect to take them off,' she said conversa-
ionally. 'And you did, didn't you?'

At last Nikolai realised that this was serious.

Very pale, he said, 'You can't believe that rubbish.'

Lisa was in anguish, as pale as he now. She waited, think-
ng, *He has to say he loves me. Nothing else will do now.*

He said, 'It's no big deal. I've bought clothes for lots of
women.'

Lisa gasped as if she had been shot.

Nikolai exclaimed at once, 'No. I didn't mean that.
Lisa—'

But she had gone.

She got home without noticing the shoppers, or the fact that
she was barefoot. In fact, if she hadn't dropped her bag on
the tallboy by the front door when they'd arrived last night
she wouldn't have found her key either.

She didn't care. She'd just had to get out of Nikolai's flat
and into her own burrow. She locked the door, unplugged
the phone and disappeared into the bath.

Her own bath preparations were simple herbal oils from
a chainstore chemist. She scrubbed herself to get rid of the
expensive scent of white lilac. Presumably he had bought
that for her to use. Before or after he seduced her? Lisa
asked herself, raging.

Oh, he had planned it like a military campaign. She wondered how many generals he had in his family tree. She
would ask him the next time she—

She stopped the thought right there. She was not going
to see him again. He had planned his last plan for the downfall of Lisa Romaine.

How certain of her he must have been. Rage dying, Lisa
cringed. This was worse than anything that Terry Long had

done to her. She had never *trusted* Terry Long. Or not as she had trusted Nikolai.

Which was when she stopped scrubbing at her skin, lay back in the bath and let the tears seep out of her eyes like blood from a wound.

She would survive. Of course she would. But just this morning she needed to let herself know the hurt before she gathered herself together and started to repair the damage Nikolai Ivanov had done.

It was one Saturday without laundry or shopping or going through the post. For once she didn't even phone her mother and Kit. If they had difficulties they would have to sort them out without Lisa this time. She needed all her courage for herself.

Eventually, of course, she had to emerge. Feeling rather as if she were recovering from flu, she went quietly out into the garden and sat under a tree. That was where Tatiana found her.

Tatiana had received a startling visit from her distraught nephew. It had only been after she had physically barred him from the outdoor staircase to Lisa's flat that he'd admitted Lisa had run away from him.

'Then go away and think about it before you try to see her again,' his fond aunt had advised him briskly.

Nikolai's eyes had been wild. 'I've got to see her.'

'Find a way to put it right first,' Tatiana had said. 'And don't think you can use me. I don't interfere between lovers.'

She'd paused hopefully. Nikolai hadn't denied it. She'd hidden a gleeful grin.

'You're on your own,' she'd informed him, and escorted him relentlessly to the front door.

Nevertheless, when she'd looked over the balcony and seen the small figure under the tree she'd gone out to join Lisa. Not interfering, she told herself. Concerned.

'Lemonade,' she said now, offering a tall glass. 'I always make my own in the summer. How was Glyndebourne?'

'Fine.' Lisa was up to politeness, but that was about all. Thank you.'

Tatiana sat down beside her companionably and crossed her legs in a double lotus that a woman half her age would have envied.

'Did Nicki do reasonable escort duty?'

Lisa gave a choke of bitter laughter. 'Beyond the call of duty.'

'Ah.' Tatiana digested this. 'He can be a bit overpowering,' she said on a questioning note.

Lisa did not respond to that at all.

'Of course, he always knows exactly what he wants,' pursued Tatiana chattily. She watched Lisa from under her eyelids. 'He said he was going to study animals when he was five. The family could not understand it. They wanted him to manage the vineyard. But he never wavered.'

Lisa shivered. It only confirmed what she had already concluded, but it was chilling. The man was single-minded. As she had proved conclusively. She had challenged him again and again. And how he had responded to her challenge!

Tatiana said, as if she were talking to herself, 'This family legend started: Nicki was serious, his brother was not. Of course they were very different. Vladi was always surrounded by girls.' She sent Lisa a quick look. 'Nicki isn't like that. He's very discriminating.'

Lisa looked at her with irony. 'Are you seriously suggesting that he doesn't get any girl that he wants?'

Tatiana had to admit that he did. 'But he respects you,' she added earnestly.

'I wind him up,' Lisa said flatly. It hurt to admit, but somehow it seemed important to say it aloud. 'I don't mean to. But there must be something about me that—' She broke off.

'Brings out the beast in him,' nodded Tatiana. She did not sound surprised.

Lisa flinched. It was much too close to the truth.

'Whatever it is, it's hell,' she said sharply. 'I suppose he's used to a different sort of girl—'

Lisa was clever, and street-smart, and she had learned a lot in the past six years. But the girls who came when Nikolai Ivanov crooked his finger were in a different class. They would be confident, well travelled: sophisticated to their well-bred bones.

'The sort of girls who wait for men to order their meals in restaurants,' she concluded, with feeling.

Tatiana was confused. 'What?'

Lisa shook her head. 'Forget it.' She got up. 'Thank you for the lemonade.'

She walked away, leaving it half drunk. Tatiana had to be content.

For the next few weeks Lisa avoided all contact with her landlady. Tatiana was quite short with Nikolai when he called from France.

And then fate took a hand.

Hurrying out of a class at the dance studio, Tatiana slipped on a newly washed floor and broke a small bone in her foot. She informed the doctor that she could not walk, must convalesce at her family home in France, and could not fly out there alone in her state of health at her age. And gave him Lisa's number at work.

Lisa dug in her bag to find the telephone number Nikolai Ivanov had given her. But when she rang it a very upper-class voice said that he was not available. It did, however, offer to pass on a message.

And Lisa received the telephone call she had been dreading that August evening.

'Lisa? You wanted to talk to me?' Nikolai sounded amazed.

His incredulity was understandable. She had refused his calls and sent back his letters unopened. He was not to be blamed if he couldn't believe that she had at last got in touch of her own volition.

The sound of his voice made Lisa start to tremble, as if

ie were in the room. Furious with herself, she gave him the
acts. Her tone was so unemotional it bordered on the in-
ulting.

There was a long silence on the other end of the line.

Eventually he said, 'What did you tell her about us?'

Lisa's heart squeezed in pain. 'That it was not a success,'
he said curtly.

This time the silence was even longer.

'I see.'

But she noticed that he didn't contradict her.

Eventually he said slowly, 'If you can bring her out here,
will send a car to meet you at Toulouse. You needn't
vorry about being forced to be pleasant to me. Tatiana will
tay with my grandparents at the château. I have my own
iouse. We needn't even see each other.'

'Oh.'

Lisa was nonplussed. Whatever she had expected the next
ime she talked to Nikolai—and her imagination had con-
ured up everything from reproaches to a full declaration of
ove—it was not this businesslike focus on the issues.

She said, 'I am very busy. I don't really have the time.'

'It need only take a weekend.'

If he had sounded as if he cared, even the slightest bit,
he would have refused. But he didn't. He sounded as if
hey had never laid in each other's arms; as if he had never
:laimed that they were not strangers; as if they would never
ouch again.

'Oh, all right,' said Lisa. 'We'll get the last plane out of
Heathrow on Friday.'

She banged the telephone down with a frustration that
she was completely unable to account for.

The turrets of the château shone like thimbles in the high
summer sun. The silver river wound through gently sloping
fields where the vines were dark pleats in the green lushness.

Riding slowly up along the river path, Nikolai looked at

the picture without seeing it. He would see her tomorrow. *Tomorrow*. And then what?

'I'll know soon,' he promised himself aloud.

The bay horse's ear twitched. He patted its neck absently.

The trouble was that Lisa was going to take one look at life here in St Aubain and hate it. It had all the things that made her jumpy and insecure: an exquisite little lodge all to himself, a seventeenth-century château, with its antiques, its library, its well-stocked stables and its inspired cuisine, and this landscape, arguably the most beautiful in France.

No, Nikolai thought ruefully. Another woman might be seduced by the beauties of his ancestral home. Lisa was going to hate it. And yet the temptation to lure her into falling in love with it was too great to resist.

So he planned his strategy quite carefully. She was going to come out here thinking that he didn't care one way or another whether he saw her at all. And when she arrived— well, he was not going to crowd her, Nikolai promised himself. This time he would be measured and sensitive. He would show her that he was prepared to share her burdens, had already found a way to help her sister. Above all he was not going to let the demands of his hot blood stampede him out of control again.

'Another plan,' he said aloud.

And wouldn't Lisa just hate *that*, if she found out? Well, hate it or not, he was desperate. So the plan had better work.

Tatiana was affronted to find that Nikolai did not meet them in person at the airport. He had appointed the village taxi driver to collect them instead. Tatiana quizzed him briskly, and ended up so angry that she forgot the wheelchair that had been provided. Instead, she limped out to the car at an Olympic pace.

'Nikolai won't be there because he's working and they've got people staying,' she flung at Lisa as soon as they were settled in the car. 'You'd think they'd realise that I'm convalescent. I need my rest. But, no. Véronique Repiquet and her new husband are down from Paris for the week.'

Lisa digested the fact that Nikolai, just as he had promised, was not at the château. She was relieved. It would have been impossible, having to be polite to him—as if they had never made wild love on his bedroom floor. This diplomatic absence of his was much the best solution from every point of view. Wasn't it?

Tatiana brooded, muttering. Lisa became aware of the cause of her displeasure.

'Don't you like—er—Véronique?'

Tatiana gave a grand shrug. 'She's stupid.'

But when they got to the château it became quickly obvious what her objection to Véronique was. It had nothing to do with the woman's IQ.

'She and Nikolai were an item, weren't they?' asked Lisa quietly as she helped Tatiana up to her room.

Lisa had been surprised at the genuine warmth of the Ivanovs' welcome. Of course they were grateful to her for helping Tatiana on her journey. But there had seemed to be more to it than that, especially when Countess Ivanova had hugged her as if she were a long-lost daughter.

Only Véronique had held aloof. And Lisa suspected she knew the reason. So she'd challenged Tatiana with it.

'Maybe once,' Tatiana admitted reluctantly.

She plumped down on the edge of the bed. Lisa took her sticks.

'Was he upset when she got married?' she asked airily, propping them up in the corner.

'Who knows what upsets Nikolai?' snapped Tatiana.

And, refusing all further offers of help, she took herself to bed in a huff.

Lisa did not fancy spending the rest of the evening in the drawing room, listening to Véronique point out obliquely that there was no room for Lisa Romaine in the world of the Ivanovs and the Repiquets. So she went to her room and tried to rest.

She had just about adjusted to Tatiana's pictures and art deco furniture. When she and Nikolai had made love, she had forgotten the antiques of his borrowed surroundings. But at the château the culture shock was total.

Lisa had been assigned a turret room. The floor was made of polished boards that creaked. There was a huge stone fireplace, filled with a great copper bowl of roses and trailing honeysuckle. And she had a four-poster bed.

She had taken one look at the huge tapestry-hung structure and blenched. It was not a bed in which anyone had ever expected to sleep alone. And somewhere out on the estate, as the Ivanovs had made perfectly clear, was the man in whose arms she had slept exquisitely.

'Damn and blast,' said Lisa, with concentrated fury. She went to bed, pulled sheets that smelled of lavender over her face, and concentrated hard on running through last month's movements in the Dow Jones index. It was a mantra that always sent her to sleep. But she had never tried it before surrounded by antique shadows, in darkness scented with beeswax polish and roses. Or with the awareness that she was in her lover's family home.

Or the certain knowledge, in every nerve and muscle and blood cell, that he was close. Somewhere.

It took several hours to get to sleep.

CHAPTER NINE

Lisa was late finding her way downstairs for breakfast. The formal rooms were empty, their priceless furniture and co-ordinating fabrics gleaming like a picture in an interior decorator's portfolio. Lisa told herself she was not intimidated and went through them, following her nose after the scent of warm croissants.

In the end she found herself in a stone-flagged kitchen. Two smiling women tried to talk to her, found she could not understand a word of French, and took her by the hand. Beaming, they led her to the swimming pool.

And Nikolai stood up to greet her.

Lisa stopped dead.

He had been swimming. Often, by the look of him, but recently enough to have left gleaming drops on his chest and darkened his hair to black. He was much browner than she remembered. *My lover*, she thought in shock. It was pure instinct, and it shook her to the core.

Lisa's heart seemed to swell until she couldn't breathe. She had known he was close. She had *known* it last night. And here he was.

She couldn't think of a thing to say.

'Hello, Lisa.' He was grave.

The women gave him a rapid debriefing. He nodded and they left.

'They've kept some rolls hot for you and they'll make some more coffee,' he translated. 'All right?'

'Thank you.' It sounded strangled.

She skirted him and sat down at a table under a wall covered with brilliant bougainvillaea.

'I—er—thought you were away.' Her voice was high with tension.

'Working,' Nikolai corrected. He sounded completely at his ease. He sat down and gave her an unshadowed smile. 'I've been in the fields since six. So I get the rest of the day off.'

'I didn't know you were a farmer.'

He doubled the wattage of his smile. Lisa felt her skin tingle with it. He's doing that deliberately, she thought with dawning indignation.

'But you don't know very much about me at all.'

'I thought we were never going to be strangers again,' she flashed.

The moment she said it Lisa realised how unwise it was. It brought back in vivid detail the sensations of that unforgettable night. She felt her colour rise helplessly. She looked away.

'So did I,' Nikolai said softly. 'So did I.'

In spite of the brilliant sun, she shivered. There was no point, she thought, in trying to avoid this. Nikolai was going to say exactly what he wanted when he felt like it. So either she spent the next two days ducking and weaving to avoid the subject or she turned and faced it now. She took a deep breath and said harshly, 'I told you once—sexual attraction can be a powerful drug. The only good thing about it is it wears off.'

'Does it?'

That, thought Lisa, was typical. And to think that she had warned him that *she* didn't play fair. When he was capable of sitting there wearing next to nothing and looking at her as if he remembered every little sensitive spot on her body. And sounding as if he *cared*.

'Yes,' she said shortly. She turned her face away.

One of the women came back with a tray. She chatted freely to Nikolai as she set the wooden table. Lisa watched. The tablecloth was lace-edged, starched and clearly an heirloom; the coffee pot was silver; the porcelain bowl for Lisa's coffee was so fine it was transparent. Lisa surveyed these collectors' items and realised that Nikolai didn't even notice them.

Here, if she needed it, was a complete illustration of the differences between them. Lisa felt something close to despair. She remembered telling Sam that she and Nikolai inhabited the same planet. How wrong could you be?

The woman poured coffee for her, gave her another nod of shining good will and left. Nikolai strolled over and sat on a stone outcrop of wall, holding a coffee cup of his own.

'What a civilised man you are,' Lisa said ironically.

She thought he would laugh, or say something clever in that slow, seductive voice. But he did not. He frowned.

'A civilised man? You mean I repress my instincts and hide my feelings?'

Lisa blinked. 'What?'

'That's what civilised behaviour is all about. Curbing the wild man within. I know all about it. That is my area of specialisation after all.'

'I would never have guessed.'

But he hardly noticed her sarcasm.

'If we weren't civilised it would be so much easier. I would read your body language. You would read mine. No room for mistakes.'

Lisa clutched her arms round herself and averted her eyes from his bare chest.

'I thought animals did all sorts of things to deceive the enemy,' she objected.

Nikolai looked down at her, the hooded eyes nearly black.

'The enemy, yes. But you and I aren't enemies.'

She looked at the Sèvres bowl. 'Aren't we?'

He went very still. 'How do I get you to trust me?' he said, almost to himself.

Lisa looked at him. His powerful shoulders were outlined against the water and, beyond, a high laurel hedge. She wanted to touch him so much it hurt. Unseen, she curled her fingers into her palms and concentrated on the picture before her. The pool glittered in the heat.

She said furiously, as much to herself as to Nikolai, 'In your dreams.'

She blundered to her feet. Only to find his body blocking hers.

He was as angry as she, but much more in control. 'You never gave me a fair hearing. You just can't bring yourself to respect a man, can you?'

Lisa's vision blurred, but she was not going to dash away tears in front of him. He had enough to gloat over already.

'Show me something to respect and I will,' she spat.

His expression softened. 'Lisa, why are we—?'

But there were voices beyond the laurel hedge.

'Damn!' he said under his breath.

The Ivanovs came into view. Along with Véronique Repiquet in designer muslin that showed off her height and her long model's legs—and her utter confidence.

'Oh,' said Countess Ivanova.

She had seen Nikolai's expression. She hesitated in the opening of the hedge.

Veronique had no such doubts. She sauntered round the pool. There she let her loose garments fall casually onto the flagstones and stood revealed in the tiniest bikini that Lisa had ever seen. It made her look like a goddess. She fluttered her fingers at Nikolai flirtatiously, ignored Lisa, and dived into the pool.

Count Ivanov bundled over to Lisa like the cavalry charging to the rescue.

'My dear, you shouldn't be out here in this sun without a hat. Let me take you inside and find one.'

He led her away before Nikolai had time to protest.

'And maybe you would like to see round the house?' he suggested as soon as they were indoors.

Lisa could only thank him. She meant it.

He was, she found, enthusiastic, but far from blind to his ancestors' faults.

'The Ivanovs always thought they were very grand, but they were terrible time-servers,' he told her, standing in front of a portrait of a large man in unconvincing military uniform. 'Feodor. Lost all his money and married a dressmaker.' He pulled a face at his ancestor. 'I assume she made the uniform from a pattern out of a storybook. Mind you, careful marriages were the secret of survival. Lots of foreign sons-in-law, in case the Tsars turned nasty. Which they did, regularly.'

He moved on down the gallery, nodding at an eighteenth-century landscape, all filigree leaves in front of a sunlit palace. Lisa peered at it. The perspective was a bit wobbly, but the painted house looked remarkably like a smaller version of the château.

'Take this place,' said the Count, confirming her suspicions. 'My ancestor was out of favour at Court. So he married off one daughter to a general of Napoleon's. And, just to make sure, another one went to a marquis of the *ancien régime*. That brought the château into the family.'

They moved on.

'Terrible old rogue he turned out to be, too,' he added ruminatively. 'Sold Versailles to a man from Massachusetts, then had to flee France when the man turned up to take possession.'

Lisa gave a choke of laughter. 'Is that true?'

'Probably. We have our share of rogues.'

He took her arm and led her round a corner where a tall Ming vase presented a hazard.

'Nicki,' he said very deliberately, 'isn't one of them.'

Lisa stopped dead so abruptly that it was clear his caution in navigating her round the heirloom had been wise.

'I'm afraid his brother was, a bit,' said Pauli sighing. 'We loved him, of course. But Vladi was not always terribly scrupulous. Especially in his dealings with women. Nicki is different.'

Lisa was uncomfortable.

'Count—'

'My dear, call me Pauli. There are too many counts in this house. Especially when all the family gets together.'

'Pauli, then. I don't think you should be talking to me about Nikolai.'

'I don't say anything behind his back I haven't said to his face,' his grandfather said reasonably. 'They were very close, Nicki and his brother, even though they were so different. When Vladi died, Nicki dropped his own life and took over Vladi's role. He's put the estate in better order than poor Vladi ever managed, I may say. He works round the clock. But he won't let anyone get close to him. It seems as if he has put a lid on his feelings and no one is going to be allowed to lift it.'

'I—'

He ignored the small, embarrassed protest.

'Mind you, I'm not saying he's a saint. He's had his girl-friends, and I'm sure one or two of them got hurt. He's as hot-blooded as the rest of the Ivanovs. Only no one has touched his heart. But he has never made promises he can't keep. And he doesn't lie.'

There was a difficult silence.

'But he *plans*,' Lisa burst out.

Pauli blinked. 'Does he?' he said, fascinated.

'All the time. And he watches me as if I'm one of his blasted animal subjects. He might as well bring his binocu-lars.'

Pauli choked, and turned it quickly into a cough.

'Um. Yes. I can see that would be very—disconcerting.' He looked at Lisa's mutinous expression and decided that he had said enough. 'Well, now, let's find you that hat.'

He found Tatiana and his wife in the rose garden.

'Either Nikolai is in love for the first time in his life or he's gone mad,' he reported. 'I've no idea what Lisa feels for him. Leave them alone.'

His wife opened her mouth.

'Nothing we can do about it,' he said sternly.

She shut it again.

'Do you promise, Marie?'

'But I like her.'

'So do I,' agreed Pauli. 'But he's a man, and he has to sort it out for himself. And if I'm any judge,' he added with glee, 'he's going to find it the hardest thing he's ever done.'

For the rest of the day either Lisa avoided Nikolai or he avoided her. She wasn't sure which. It meant that she braced herself for war every time a footstep came down one of the raked paths or a door opened. War never came.

She went to bed with a tearing headache and lay awake between her tapestries for most of the hot night. Every time she closed her eyes she could feel Nikolai watching her, his breath against her skin. And then she opened her eyes again and she was alone.

'I'm going mad,' she moaned.

She gave up on sleep as soon as it was light and slipped out of the château. There was a hill to the east of the park, and she just kept walking towards it. The sun rose, pulling a heat haze off the dewy ground. Soon Lisa began to sweat.

She pulled off her cotton sweater and tied it round her waist, leaving her arms and throat bare to the now burning sun. The ground climbed. She thought she heard a river, and thirsted for water. But she didn't know how far below it was, and all the time something urged her on.

And then she pulled herself up over a rise at the very top of the hill and saw it below her! There indeed was a river, curling lazily through the valley like a strip of silver ribbon. And on the opposite bank a walled castle, all rose-red stone and turrets, like a picture from a medieval Book of Hours.

Lisa forgot she was tired and thirsty. She sank onto the dusty earth and stared at the little magic fortress. Suddenly, sharply, she wanted Nikolai to be here, sharing it. She wanted him so badly she thought he must hear her thoughts.

'Nonsense,' she told herself. 'Too much walking in the sun without a hat.'

But she was not really surprised when she heard a horse'
hooves.

Nikolai came bursting through the trees and leaped off th
horse. Lisa didn't move. Even when he looped the reins ove
a bush and strode towards her she just sat there, as if she wa
expecting him, smiling at him dreamily.

Nikolai knelt down beside her, his eyes hard with anxiety
'Are you all right?'

'I wanted you to see this,' she said, as if she were excusin
an inopportune phone call.

Nikolai cast an impatient look across the valley.

'Yes, beautiful, I'll buy you a postcard,' he said with su
preme indifference. 'Why on earth did you wander off lik
that? I thought something had happened to you.'

Lisa tipped back her head and smiled straight into his eyes
'I think it has.'

'What?' He leaned forward, searching her face. Gently h
pushed back her hair, so that he could look into her eye
without interruption. 'Are you *sure* you're all right?' H
sounded worried.

'I was sitting here wanting you. And here you are.' Lis
was smug. 'Of course I'm all right.'

Nikolai shook his head. 'You shouldn't say things like tha
if you don't mean them,' he said, half-laughing, half-serious
He slid an arm round her waist and tried to help her to he
feet. 'Can't you stand?'

Lisa laughed up at him. 'Make me,' she said naughtily.

'Oh, *Lisa*,' It was a groan. 'Did you have anything to ea
before you left?'

She shook her head.

'Or drink?' He sounded despairing.

'Not since last night.'

'Right. The first thing you need is several litres of water.
He began hauling her to her feet, looking at the horse with
a considering eye. 'Do you ride?'

''Course I do, Count. Doesn't everybody? Buses and rol

ercoasters a speciality,' said Lisa. It struck her as exquisitely amusing. She said it again. She couldn't stop laughing.

Nikolai sent her a harassed look. He got her up and locked an arm round her. Then he unhooked the bridle and began to scramble them all haphazardly down the slope between the trees. The horse, much better behaved than Lisa, followed obediently. By contrast Lisa kept wanting Nikolai to stop and kiss her. She said so several times.

'One day—' said Nikolai between his teeth, tried almost beyond endurance.

But then the slope lessened and Lisa caught sight of his goal. It was a small lake, fed by the rushing stream she had heard earlier. Nikolai marched her to the bank and dropped her unceremoniously. Then he knelt and caught some water in his cupped hands.

'Drink,' he said curtly.

She did. It made her realise how thirsty she was. She knelt and drank avidly, straight from the stream. The water was so cold it set her teeth tingling. But it was like wine.

Eventually she raised her head. It was like coming out of a dream. Or rather a nightmare, in which she had made a public fool of herself.

'Ow,' she said, with feeling.

Nikolai was rather pale, in spite of his outdoor tan. 'You were dehydrated. It does odd things to people. Don't worry about it. You weren't responsible for anything you said.'

'But—' Lisa fell over the words. She felt crippled by shyness. 'Oh, hell!'

She looked at the lake. It was in a clearing, the trees gold with the satiated excess of summer. Filtered sunbeams struck green rainbows off the leaves. Willow branches hung into the water. But the surface was a dark mirror, an alternative universe below the still water, showing a silent landscape and two unspeaking figures turning to each other.

At the bank, the water lapped gently. Out on the little lake a breeze riffled the water into movement. But the shadow

landscape stayed still. And so did Lisa and Nikolai. Neithe
spoke.

Lisa thought, *I want him. I need him. I can't just stan
here not telling him.* But shyness locked her tongue as if sh
were a schoolgirl on her first date. She despised herself from
her heart. But there was not a thing she could do about it
And Nikolai made no move to help her.

At last he said in a constrained voice, 'I must take yo
back. You've obviously overtired yourself.'

She thought, *He doesn't want me.*

He had to know what she wanted. Heaven knows, on tha
scramble down the wooded hillside she had told him plainl
enough. But his grandfather had said he didn't make promise
he couldn't keep. Presumably that included not letting womel
who had fallen in love with him burn their boats when h
didn't love them in return.

She said with a painful smile, 'Not only civilised, an hon
ourable man.'

Nikolai closed his eyes, as if he was in pain. 'Lisa—'

But she had turned away. 'I think you're right. I feel ver
strange. Take me home.'

He put her on the horse and led them back to the châtea
without further argument.

Lisa was put straight to bed by her concerned hostess. Sh
slept heavily through the sultry afternoon, but was eventuall
persuaded down to join the party for drinks by the pool.

She saw at once that Nikolai wasn't there. Véronique was
however, her muslins transformed for the cocktail hour by
the addition of several gold chains and rings.

'If you're looking for the heart-throb, he's gone off to se
some boffin,' said Véronique. She was plainly not pleased
'Some Englishman he knows from his research who is havin
a holiday round here. You'd think it could wait—especiall
as Edmond has come to take me back to Paris this evening
But, no!'

'The man rang him. He said he had the answer to Nikolai'

question,' said Countess Ivanova temperately. She patted Lisa's hand. 'Are you feeling better, my dear?'

'I'm fine,' lied Lisa.

She thought she would never be fine again. This was worse than when Terry had left.

Because I wasn't in love with Terry, she thought suddenly. The implications of that made her start to shake.

She accepted the champagne cocktail that Pauli gave her. But she didn't touch it. She listened to the lively conversation between their hosts and various other guests from the locality. Even when it was in English it made no sense to her.

I'm in love with Nikolai Ivanov.

It was wonderful. It was terrible. It was hopeless.

Lisa sat very still and hugged the knowledge to her at the same time as she acknowledged that it was quite, quite useless. Still, he had held her. She had made love with him. She would know love for the rest of her life.

When Véronique's husband came and sat beside her, Lisa looked up, her eyes shy and yet filled with such tender joy that it made him blink.

'We haven't met,' he said. 'Edmond Le Brun.' They shook hands. 'I gather you're a bond trader.'

He was a nice man. He brought her out, asked her questions about her work. Soon she was talking freely, making them all laugh. Herself again. Well, nearly.

'It sounds very stressful,' said Pauli. 'How do people stand it?'

'Drink, mostly,' said Lisa coolly. 'Some drugs. Crazy partying is obligatory. But the really hot traders get a buzz out of it that's better than all the drink, drugs and parties together.'

'And are you a "hot trader"?' asked Véronique. Her voice was edged with spite.

Lisa grinned. 'I am this year.'

'And do you use drink and drugs?' she drawled. 'Or is the buzz of success enough?'

'She dances,' said a voice out of the darkness.

Lisa's heart turned a slow, dangerous somersault and came to rest somewhere in the region of her toes.

Nikolai strolled forward. He was wearing dark trousers and an open necked cream shirt. Lisa looked at the strong brown column of his throat and was engulfed by lust.

He smiled down at her, his eyes a stranger's. Lisa's heart went into retreat.

'Dances like a dervish and fights like a fiend. Which, to be fair, she warned me about. Isn't that right, Lisa?'

'Right,' she said gaily, bravely.

Her heart crept under a stone and stayed there.

No one seemed to notice. Nikolai's arrival had added spice to the party. The noise level rose. Twilight closed in. A buffet was set out, wine flowed. Someone put on some music.

Véronique drifted over.

'We have to be going,' she said, though her husband was doing an athletic merengue with the publisher daughter of a local landowner. 'So nice to have met you. Will you be here for the harvest?'

Lisa shook her head. 'Shouldn't think so.'

'Oh, that's a shame. It's a real crowd-puller.'

Lisa smiled with an effort. 'Really? Very traditional, is it?'

Véronique gave a husky chuckle. 'The best tradition is the sight of Nicki stripping off and mucking in with the workers. Scrumptious. Women come from miles.'

Lisa flinched. She knew that Véronique was spiteful, and she knew that she was possessive of Nikolai. But there was still enough in the nasty little remark to hurt. *She's telling me I'm just another pathetic groupie,* Lisa thought. The trouble was, Véronique was probably right. Though Nikolai was too civilised to say so.

She looked up and saw him in the light of the newly lit candles. He was watching her, his face grave. Lisa couldn't bear it.

She raised her voice slightly. 'I only came to help Tatiana. I don't fit in here and I don't want to. I won't be back.'

He turned away.

CHAPTER TEN

LISA did not see Nikolai again. She left quite deliberately before he had come up from his own house in the morning. That, she reasoned, would spare them both embarrassment. And worse than embarrassment.

After yesterday, by the lake, she was almost certain that he knew she loved him. He was too experienced to have missed it, even if she hadn't known it herself. And he had made it plain that he was not going to take it further.

Lisa thought she understood him very well. She even admired him, in a tortured sort of way. For him, a night in bed with a lady who knew the score was one thing. Kissing a woman vulnerable with unrequited love for him was something quite different. Oh, yes, in his own way, Nikolai Ivanov was an honourable man.

'Makes a change for you to be breaking your heart over an honourable man,' Lisa told her reflection in Countess Ivanova's cheval glass. She was trying hard to be bracing. 'All you've got to do now is get over him.'

She certainly did her best in the next couple of weeks. To her inexpressible relief there was an emergency meeting of Napier Kraus chief traders in New York. Then a conference was put together in Sydney to discuss the East Asia crisis. Lisa went.

Nikolai worked like a demon, putting the estate paperwork and maintenance plan in order for when he was in Borneo. When he wasn't working he was preparing for the expedition. Eventually he announced that he was going to London to meet the rest of Sedgewick's team.

'Oh?' said his grandfather. He had been expecting this, though he wouldn't have admitted it to anyone, not even his wife.

Nikolai looked at him narrowly.

'They have all been on expedition together before. The only one I've been with is Pinero. We need to do some training together.'

'Of course you do.'

'You're an old fox,' he informed his grandfather, undeceived. 'All right. Lisa has gone off the loop again. Won't answer any of my messages. Her office says she's been away, but she's due back this week. God knows if she'll talk to me.'

'What are you going to do if she won't?' asked his grandfather, interested. He had never seen Nikolai like this.

White teeth flashed in the tanned face. 'Hunt like I've never hunted before.'

Pauli believed him.

It was the weekend of the Notting Hill Carnival. Barriers were going up to mark out the route of the big procession and there was a buzz of anticipation. The smart Palladian streets emptied as many residents left for the long weekend, to get away from the noise of a two-day street party that boasted it was the largest outside the Caribbean. Well, in Europe anyway.

And what would Lisa do? Nikolai couldn't make up his mind. Party? Well he had seen her do that. Or run from the fun? He had seen her do that too.

She was still not answering her telephone. So he rented a car and took up a look-out post in her street. With so many residents in flight he had never found parking so easy.

Lisa got off the plane from Sydney and went straight to her mother's house. There had been a panic-stricken phone call at four in the morning. It would have taken a harder heart than Lisa's to ignore it.

Joanne was sitting at the table—still strewn with the debris of several days, from the look of it. She didn't answer the bell and she didn't get up when Lisa let herself in with the key from under the flowerpot.

'Kit's gone,' she announced tragically.

Lisa's temper snapped. 'Thank you, yes, it was a good flight. And, no, I'm not in the least tired.'

'What?'

Lisa gentled. 'Snap out of it, Mum,' she said wearily. 'Kit isn't a child any more. Where has she gone?'

'That man—' Joanne shed angry tears.

Lisa made a cup of tea. 'Which man?' she said patiently. 'Are we talking about the college stud again?'

Joanne lifted her head and glared. 'That man *you* brought into our lives. Nick Ivanov, or whatever he calls himself.'

'Nikolai?' Lisa's head was beginning to spin. 'How do you know Nikolai Ivanov?'

'He came here, saying he knew someone who was doing research on Kit's problem. I didn't want her to talk to him. I said it could be dangerous. But the self-help group said they had heard of him and he was respectable, there weren't any drugs or anything involved. And all the time he was trying to take her away from us—' Her voice became suspended.

Lisa was very pale. 'Who was trying to take her away from us? Nikolai?'

'No, this friend of his. Professor Something-or-other. He says all she needs is to be independent. When you know—'

And Joanne burst into a flood of tears.

'All right. All right.' Lisa patted her mother's back. 'Are you saying that Kit has run off with this Professor?'

'No. She's got a job,' said Joanne, in tones of despair. 'She left me a note.'

She brought it out of her pocket. Judging by the folds and stains, it had been read many times. Lisa scanned it rapidly.

'This sounds OK,' she said at last. 'She's staying with a

friend. She'll get in touch when she has somewhere permanent.' She looked at the date. 'Mum, she only went three days ago. Has she called?'

'Yes, but—'

'Then stop worrying,' Lisa said firmly. 'She'll be fine.'

'You'll look for her, won't you? Find her. Make her come home.' Joanne was frantic.

Lisa looked at her mother and had a revelation. Kit had been living with the pressure of this suffocating love for years. No wonder she had withdrawn. Why had Lisa not seen it?

'I'll go home first,' she hedged. 'She's probably left me a message.' Lisa helped her mother to her feet and guided her towards the stairs. 'Why don't you have a bath while I get this cleared up? You'll feel better afterwards.'

Joanne did.

By the time Lisa had returned the dining room and kitchen to its normal order she was exhausted. She fell asleep in the minicab taking her home. Which was why she didn't notice the car and its occupant sitting outside Tatiana's house.

Nikolai was nearly asleep himself. He had been relaxing his muscles with practised care for some hours. He knew the dangers of cramp during a long wait. He often had to wait for hours in the jungle before the animal he was studying came into view. He knew how to do it only too well: stillness and patience were the key.

So he remained still and patient when he saw Lisa haul her suitcase up the front steps. He didn't get out of the car until his quarry had committed herself and the front door was open. Then he ran, silent as a shadow.

She swung round, alarmed. But jet lag and extended housework had taken their toll. She was too slow. Nikolai shut the door behind him.

'You and I,' he said, 'need to talk.'

Lisa's temper was already frayed. Now it snapped.

'Are you a control freak, or what?' she yelled. 'Get out of my house.'

'This is where I came in,' he murmured. 'Tatiana's house. I have a key now, if necessary.'

'Don't patronise me,' said Lisa, near to inexplicable tears. 'I can't bear men who patronise me.'

He shook his head. 'How can you possibly say I'm patronising you?'

'You see. There you go again.' She was so angry she could hardly get the words out. 'I suppose it's culture shock. You can't have met too many people as far removed from your social sphere as me.'

Nikolai's eyes sharpened. 'You mean I'd do better with you if I put you down, like that thug we met at Glyndebourne?' he whipped back. 'Or the boss who is so jealous of you he can't see straight? Yet you keep eating your heart out for him, don't you? Is that it? You like men who treat you badly?'

'No one,' said Lisa, shaking with temper, 'has ever treated me as badly as you have.'

She advanced on him, tears streaming down her face. She was quite unaware of it.

'You manipulated me from the start. You spied on me. You tricked me into wearing your damned dress. All because you had this plan to get me into bed.'

Nikolai was blank. 'Plan—? What are you talking about?'

Lisa gave a scream. 'You *told* me. You said you'd been promising it to yourself for weeks, you bastard.'

'Oh, good God—is that what this nonsense is all about? I only meant—'

But Lisa wasn't giving him any more time.

'Get out,' she said pantingly. 'Get out now. You're a cheat and a liar and I don't want to see you ever again.'

Nikolai was now as angry as she was.

'Don't worry. I'm going. No wonder you don't respect men if they let you get away with tantrums like this.'

He slammed the front door behind him.

Lisa sagged against it and cried until she had no tears left. In the morning she found that the answering machine was full. Most of the messages were from Nikolai, increasing in urgency. She wiped them all. And one message was from Kit.

If Kit hadn't left her name, Lisa thought, she wouldn't have recognised her. Her sister's voice bubbled with vitality. Everything was great and she was going to come round on Sunday morning and take Lisa out for lunch to celebrate.

'Sunday?' Lisa looked wildly at the calendar. 'Today! Oh, help.'

She hadn't even unpacked her case, or touched the washing she had brought back. Already it was too late. The doorbell was ringing.

Kit took one horrified look at Lisa's wretched expression and caught her in a bear hug.

'What's *wrong*?'

Lisa told her. There didn't seem much point in keeping it a secret. It was going to scar her life after all.

But Kit didn't seem to enter into her feelings with the unquestioning sisterly support she'd expected.

'I thought he was nice.'

Lisa glared. Then the fight went out of her and she blew her nose. 'He's wonderful,' she muttered.

'Well, then, see him. Talk to him. Explain. He's not unreasonable.'

'Oh, yes, he is,' said Lisa, firing up. She blew her nose again. 'Anyway, that's not the point. He doesn't love me. That's the bottom line, Kit. He's the most sophisticated man in Europe. I just don't begin to measure up. There's no way round that.'

Kit couldn't think of anything to say.

Still jet lagged, Lisa went to bed early. Concerned, Kit offered to stay the night.

'At least I can do your washing for you,' she said. 'And bring you breakfast in bed tomorrow.'

'Thank you,' said Lisa, touched.

She was asleep as soon as her head touched the pillow. So

she didn't hear the bell ring. Or Kit answer it. Or any of the low-voiced conversation that followed.

Kit found herself torn. On the one hand her first loyalty was, inevitably, to Lisa. On the other she didn't think Nikolai was the manipulative snob that Lisa had painted. And, strongest of all, she had the nasty feeling that it was Lisa's financial support of herself and her mother which had caused much of the original misunderstanding. Nikolai would never have been so suspicious if Lisa hadn't seemed to be unaccountably penniless.

So Kit compromised. She would not let him into the flat. And she certainly would not wake Lisa. But she followed him through Tatiana's sitting room into the garden and listened.

'The trouble is, she doesn't believe you're really interested in her,' she said, when Nikolai had finished.

He stared. 'How can she not believe it?'

'Well, you see, there was someone else once,' said Kit uncomfortably. 'He didn't think she was good enough for him.'

Nikolai swore. Then the most sophisticated man in Europe, the jet set's most eligible bachelor, turned to Kit Romaine with a look bordering on despair.

'Help me, Kit.'

Lisa couldn't understand why Kit insisted on going to the Carnival. It didn't seem like her retiring sister at all.

But— 'I want to see the floats,' said Kit with determination.

It was afternoon when they made their way towards the party. Lisa wore one of her short flared skirts and a backless black jersey that clung. Kit borrowed a tee shirt and shorts and tried to look as relaxed as Lisa.

The first thing they heard were the whistles, dozens of them, all on different notes. Then, as they got closer to the Carnival route, there were the sound systems, heavy with bass, playing everything from reggae to heavy metal, with more than a seasoning of salsa. In spite of the fact that her heart was broken, Lisa's hips began to rotate to the rhythm.

Kit was wide-eyed. She danced a little, ate a lot of Caribbean specialities— 'I think callaloo must be some sort of spinach,' she announced, wiping hot chili sauce off her chin with only moderate success—and finally forgot that she had no confidence and disappeared with a party of steel band groupies.

Lisa grinned, and picked up a can of cola. The shadows were lengthening and the press of people made the streets stuffy. Five guys in fringed trousers waved to her from a slow-rolling float. They shook their maracas in a naughty salute. Lisa waggled her hips in friendly acknowledgement, but her heart wasn't in it. She began to drift homeward.

She was away from the crowd, in the diamond-hard heat of an empty terrace, when she heard a voice behind her, low, sexy and husky with laughter. She knew that voice.

'I'd know that butterfly tattoo anywhere.'

She stopped dead, not turning round. She had, she realised, been half waiting for this all day. She straightened her spine and began to march—there was no other word for it—up the road.

Nikolai caught up easily. 'Come and dance with me?'

He was, Lisa saw with indignation, wearing ragged denim shorts and no shirt at all. She averted her eyes hurriedly and didn't answer. He side-slipped beside her, chuckling.

'All right. Then marry me?'

Lisa glared. 'Go away and find someone else to laugh at.'

She saw the gate to the gardens ahead. Tatiana had given her a key which she had never used. Well, this was where she found out whether it worked. She twisted the thong round her wrist and fished out her keyring.

The key worked. She was not, however, fast enough to stop Nikolai following her in.

The perimeter of white terraces, embroidered with lacy ironwork balconies, gleamed. The garden they enclosed was silent in the dusty sun. Headily scented roses blew among ivy and jasmine and the first goldening of wisteria leaves. Out on the green velvet lawn, trees were filled with the last surge of summer foliage: fire-dark copper beech, sturdy sycamores and slim silver birch. And in the hot afternoon not a leaf moved.

'No one about,' he said approvingly. 'Everyone fled to the country?'

Lisa didn't answer him. He kept pace with her.

'Lisa.' He wasn't laughing any more. 'Where did I go wrong?'

She swung round on him. 'The first day we met,' she said intensely. 'Stop pretending. *Please.*'

Nikolai frowned. 'Pretending what?'

'I'm not your class and we both know it. Hell, you even said it.'

He was outraged. 'I didn't.'

'You said I wasn't feminine,' Lisa shouted at him.

It cost him a moment's thought, but he did, eventually, remember. 'But that was ages ago. Right at the start. Did it seem to you that I thought you were unfeminine when we went to Glyndebourne?'

Lisa flushed, and began to walk rapidly towards Tatiana's house.

'That was different.'

'I'm glad you noticed,' said Nikolai grimly

'But you didn't want me in France. By the lake—' Lisa choked and folded her lips together, frowning mightily. She did not abate her pace.

Nikolai put a hand on her shoulder and swung her round to face him.

'In France you were half out of your head with dehydration. Did you think I would jump on you when you weren't yourself? Even if you wanted me to?'

Colour flooded into Lisa's cheeks. 'I didn't. I *didn't.* I—'

But he caught her so her feet were off the ground by a few inches, holding her against his naked chest so that she could feel the way his heart galloped.

'Be very careful,' he said harshly. 'I'm coming to the end of my stock of chivalrous restraint.'

'You wouldn't be restrained if you loved me,' Lisa yelled, struggling.

'Oh?' He held her for a moment. Then, very slowly and deliberately, he picked her up.

'What are you doing?'

'Losing my head,' said Nikolai calmly.

He was making his way purposefully towards a small clearing. It was protected by a tall hedge of old roses, overblown in their pink and gold luxuriance and heavy with fragrance. Lisa beat at his chest.

'Oh, you think everything is a joke. I hate you. I *hate* you.'

'No, you don't,' he said, slipping into the clearing and taking her down with him onto the secluded bank of moss and grasses. His hands were passionate, his voice thickening. 'You fancy me something rotten.'

'*Oh!*'

'And it's entirely mutual. Time we stopped fighting it,' said Nikolai, suddenly no longer calm.

His tongue probed her mouth ruthlessly. Lisa fought him even as her head reeled with excitement. Nikolai's hands slid under the cotton top, finding her nipples with precision. Ignoring her furious protest, he brought them to insistent, stinging life. Lisa moaned.

Neither could have said at what point they stopped fighting. But they were not fighting when Lisa contorted herself round him, when she tried to cover every inch of warm tanned skin with kisses, plucking at his shorts, her hand restlessly seeking his pulsing hardness. Or when Nikolai held her away from him and said fiercely, 'Marry me!'

'Nikolai,' she moaned, tortured.

He said between his teeth, 'Marriage, or I take you home this minute.'

Lisa wriggled against him challengingly. 'Oh yeah?'

His eyes closed in near anguish at the temptation. But his resolution did not waver.

'Marriage or nothing.'

She paused, wicked hands still for a moment.

'But marriage is for life,' she said uncertainly.

He opened his eyes. They were golden and full of tender laughter. More than laughter. *Love*. Or something like love. And she had seen that look before, Lisa realised blankly.

'It is indeed,' he said gently.

'But I'm not your type. I don't belong in your world,' Lisa said, shocked into revealing her deepest fears. 'You think I'm loud and rude and I get up your nose.'

He moved against her in silent, explicit answer.

Lisa's eyes flared. But she said with bitter honesty, 'Terry Long wasn't a count with ancestors, and even he knew I was trash.'

Nikolai's expression grew violent.

'Never,' he said between rigid lips, 'say anything like that again.'

Lisa met his eyes.

'I have wanted you since the first day I saw you,' Nikolai said raggedly.

Holding his eyes, Lisa began to wriggle her way out of clothes that were suddenly too confining, in spite of their summer lightness. Nikolai watched. Then pushed aside her skirt, gently but purposefully, and pulled her on top of him, flesh to demanding flesh.

'And I want you now so badly it hurts,' he told her, racked.

They held off no longer. They drove each other, wilder and harder, demanding and responding until Lisa sobbed aloud. But what shook her was Nikolai's total surrender to the tempest. He shouted aloud. Trembling, triumphant, Lisa strained him to her. The tempest went nuclear.

Later—a long time later—he tidied her clothes, kissed her hair and told her she had now burned her boats.

'But—'

'And no more nonsense about not being feminine,' said Nikolai commandingly. 'Any more feminine and I'd die.'

EPILOGUE

It was a brilliant wedding, everyone agreed. There were roses instead of lilies, a salsa combo instead of an orchestra, and nobody went home when the beat hotted up. The bride wore a simple medieval dress that had come straight out of a family Book of Hours and was, it was said, the personal choice of the bridegroom.

It was quite possible. All brides looked beautiful, by definition. But this one looked as if someone had lit a light inside her. Well, it was understandable. The former most eligible bachelor in Europe never left her side, not even to dance with his grandmother.

The photographers went home well satisfied.

Countess Ivanova whispered in her husband's ear, 'I told you the Repiquet wedding was good practice. I'd never have got it done if I hadn't had all those names and numbers.'

Her husband could have said, but did not, that he didn't think either Nikolai or Lisa would have cared an iota. He patted her hand.

As the September shadows lengthened over the vineyard, Lisa let her head drop onto Nikolai's shoulder. A scented breeze stirred her hair. The first stars were out.

'I feel as if I belong now,' she said softly.

His arm tightened. 'Yes.'

'I didn't before. Not at home. Not at work. It was sort of lonely.'

'I know.'

She looked up at that. There was something in his voice. 'You too?'

'Of course.'

186

'So...' unbelievably, she was still shy '...do you belong with me, then?'

His arm tightened so hard it hurt. 'For as long as I live,' he said in a low voice.

Lisa sighed contentedly. She knew him now. She could, she thought, trust him for the rest of her life. What did it matter if Nikolai couldn't bring himself to say it out loud?

Nikolai cleared his throat like an unpractised public speaker.

He said, as he had said once before, though she hadn't heard him, 'Lisa, darling.'

Not quite knowing why, the bride held her breath.

'I love you,' said Nikolai with painful intensity.

Under the starlit sky it was a vow.

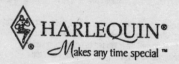